OLIVER'S
GREAT BIG
UNIVERSE

OLIVER'S GREAT BIG UNIVERSE

BY JORGE CHAM

AMULET BOOKS • NEW YORK

Library of Congress Control Number 2023933389

ISBN 978-1-4197-6408-0

Text and illustrations © 2023 Jorge Cham
Edited by Howard W. Reeves
Book design by Chelsea Hunter

Printed and bound in U.S.A.
10 9 8 7 6 5 4 3 2

ABRAMS The Art of Books
195 Broadway, New York, NY 10007
abramsbooks.com

To the best mom in the universe
—Oliver

CONTENTS

CHAPTER 1
GAMMA RAYS FROM SPACE

HELLO.

I know what you're thinking. What makes an average eleven-year-old kid like me qualified to tell you anything about the universe?

ME →

JUST FINISHED FIFTH GRADE.

LIKES:
• BOOKS
• COMICS

~~AWESOME~~ NOT BAD AT VIDEO GAMES.

THAT'S ABOUT IT.

Am I a famous scientist? No.

Am I a super-genius at everything? Not really.

There are definitely smarter kids than me. Take Christopher, for example. He once solved a Rubik's Cube in 12.7 seconds for the school talent show. Blindfolded.

MY IMPRESSED FACE. →

AHHH!!

Or Zubi. She once wrote the whole history of the battles of the American Revolution for a three-page class writing assignment.

YOUR HANDWRITING IS SO . . . SMALL.

YOU SAID THREE PAGES.

In fact, there are a lot of talented kids in my class.

ZOE C.
PRO SOCCER
PLAYER

MATEO S.
AMAZING
ARTIST

GABBY M.
CLASS
PRESIDENT

PTHBHT
PTHBHT!

SVEN P.
CAN USE HIS ARMPIT
LIKE A MUSICAL
INSTRUMENT

Me? Let's just say my elementary school principal
knew me by my first name and I saw the inside of
her office more than a typical kid my age should.

HELLO AGAIN, OLIVER.

PRINCIPAL NARRO

But I digress. That's a fancy word for the fact that I get distracted a lot. You'll probably notice that when reading this book.

Sometimes I get distracted while I'm distracted. Like right now, I'm supposed to be practicing piano, but instead I'm writing this book. Except that instead of writing this book, I just spent the last fifteen minutes reading a comic book.

NOT WRITING THIS BOOK.

ME →

THIS BOOK. →

. . . OR PLAYING PIANO.

But back to the topic. I do pay attention some-times, and I totally paid attention on a very special day at the end of fifth grade.

DR. HOWARD'S PRESENTATION

Throughout the year, Mrs. Howard (our teacher) had brought grown-ups in to talk to us about their jobs. Like one time, Devon's grandpa came to tell us about being a geologist. Did you know you can spend your whole life studying just rocks?

Or another time, Alejandro's mom came to tell us about her job as a veterinarian, which is an animal doctor. She showed us a bunch of gross pictures of pets she's cured, which was a disaster because it was right after lunch.

Anyway, near the end of the school year, Dr. Howard came to class to talk to us about what he does. At first, I thought it was funny that he had the same last name as our teacher, until I realized they are actually married. I was shocked.

TEACHERS ARE PEOPLE, TOO!
(SHOCKING!)

THEY:
- ARE NOT ROBOTS (OR ALIENS)
- HAVE FAMILIES AND STUFF!
- PROBABLY READ COMIC BOOKS WHEN THEY WERE KIDS (AND MAY STILL READ THEM!)
- COULD STILL BE ALIENS (I CAN'T SAY FOR SURE THEY ARE NOT)

Dr. Howard came to talk to us about GAMMA RAYS. It turns out he's not a regular doctor, like my ex-friend (more on that later) José's parents, who give people checkups or take out their tonsils or anything. Dr. Howard is a science doctor.

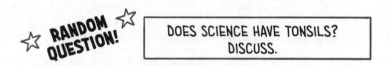

☆ RANDOM QUESTION! ☆

DOES SCIENCE HAVE TONSILS?
DISCUSS.

According to Dr. Howard, gamma rays are a kind of light that can come from space. Sometimes a star will explode and send out this kind of light, and it's so bright and powerful that if it hit Earth, it would totally fry us.

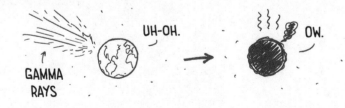

UH-OH.

GAMMA RAYS

OW.

Poof, just like that. The rays would blow away all the air on Earth and burn everything to a crisp.

But then Dr. Howard also said gamma rays are pretty cool. If they don't happen to hit us directly, or if they're not that powerful, they can actually tell us a lot about the universe and all the different things in it, like stars, or black holes, or even if there's life on other planets.

That's when I knew: I want to be an astrophysicist when I grow up. That's the kind of science doctor

Dr. Howard is. I mean, I may not grow up to be a famous soccer player or win any art contests, but maybe I can be like Dr. Howard and study the universe.

MAYBE THAT'S MY TALENT!

Yup, that's totally for me. To look up at the sky and figure out how all the stars and galaxies in the universe work, or how planets crash into each other, or how far away aliens from outer space might be. Yessiree, I'm going to be Dr. Oliver, astrophysicist, someday.

ME, IN THE FUTURE (MAYBE)

DR. OLIVER

Well, that or an actor. That's my other career option. I've never been in a play or in any movies, but I'm pretty good at doing accents. Like I can do a really awesome Scottish accent.

I'M DOING ONE RIGHT NOW!

So that got me thinking: What *else* don't I know about the universe? What other cool stuff is out there in space? It turns out, a LOT. Dr. Howard says the universe is HUGE, and it's full of weird and wacky things like:

Aliens (probably): Dr. Howard thinks there are so many planets out there, there must be at least with aliens on it. Imagine if we met them one day!

WANT TO HEAR MY SCOTTISH ACCENT?

Black Holes: Black holes are holes in space that you can't ever get out of. Sort of like a comfy couch on a rainy day.

 Invisible Stuff: Dr. H. says there are all kinds of invisible stuff in the universe, from big blobs the size of galaxies to super-tiny particles that are zooming through us right now.

I told Dr. Howard of my plan to be an astrophysicist, and, needless to say, he was *very* excited.

OK, it took some convincing, but eventually he said he was going to try to teach me more stuff. Then I had an awesome idea: I would write it all down and tell *other* kids about it in a book. I figure what better way to learn than by explaining it to someone else (you)? That's what my dad always says: The best way to know something is to explain it. And he's usually only wrong half the time.

Who knows, maybe after reading this, you'll want to be an astrophysicist, too (or an actor).

Also, what if you do meet an alien one day, and all they want to talk about is the universe? I'm guessing we won't have a lot in common with them. I mean, they probably don't watch the same TV shows or read the same comic books we do, so if you ever run into them, you'll be glad to have this book to talk about.

Otherwise, it's going to be aaawwwwkwaaarrd.

CHAPTER 2
THE BIG BANG!

OK, so if I'm going to tell you about the universe, I should probably start at the beginning.

You know how sometimes at school they squeeze everybody together for school assembly or events and it feels like things are about to explode?

For example, soon after I met Dr. Howard I got caught in the "Narrows." That's what everyone calls the cramped hallway on the way to the cafeteria at my old elementary school. There's always a pileup there when the lunch bell rings, but on that particular day, things were extra cramped because it was Potato Tot Friday and Stevie Rozecki was complaining about the potato tots.

Stevie complaining about the cafeteria food isn't anything new. But that day Ms. Chen, our lunch lady, wasn't having any of it.

So we were all squeezed in the hallway waiting and waiting, and as we waited, more and more kids kept coming. Then things started to get really stuffy and hot when the smell of the potato tots began to seep into the hallway. Everyone got restless and hungry.

Now, it would have all been fine, except that Roger Chung just happened to utter those four fateful words:

And then, BOOM.

Everyone exploded out of the hallway faster than you can say, "He who smelt it, dealt it." Suddenly, nobody cared about the potato tots.

AHHH!

AHHH!

RUN!!

OK, now keep that picture in your mind, because that's how the universe began. Not with a fart, but with a bang.

Dr. Howard says that when the universe started, all the stuff that we can see, all the stars and planets and asteroids and galaxies and stuff, all of that was super squished together. How squished together? Imagine trying to squeeze all that stuff into a space smaller than this dot:

I know, it's hard to believe all the stuff in the known universe could be squished so small, but that's how it was.

And actually, Dr. Howard says I'd have to draw a dot that was a million times smaller to really show how squished the universe was. Unfortunately, I don't have a marker that thin, so you'll just have to use your imagination.

Then the universe exploded. One second, the universe was super squished together, and the next, BANG! It was HUGE.

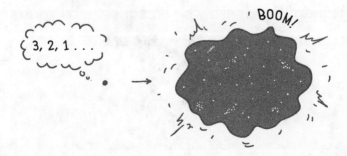

Dr. Howard says this happened about fourteen billion years ago (or 14,000,000,000 years if you like zeros), which is a long time ago. I checked and the dinosaurs were around starting only about 240 million years ago (240,000,000 years), so this was WAY before that.

Now, I know what you're thinking. How do we know about something that happened so long ago? I can't even remember what I did two weeks ago!

Then Dr. Howard said something that really blew my mind. He said we know the universe exploded because it is STILL exploding today. Whaaaaaa??

WE'RE LIVING IN AN EXPLOSION??

DID I JUST EXPLODE YOUR MIND?

He said that if you look up at all the galaxies in the sky with a telescope (a galaxy is a big group of stars like the one we live in, which is called the Milky Way), you'll notice something weird: All the galaxies are moving AWAY from each other.

SEE YA!

HEY, WAIT UP!

I'M OUTTA HERE.

BYE!

Now, if you see a bunch of galaxies moving away from each other, you have to figure that they were probably all together at some point, and that's how scientists first came up with the idea that the universe was once really squished together.

NOW

BEFORE

It's like what I imagine my old principal, Dr. Narro, thought when she stepped into the hallway and saw a bunch of kids running away from each other that day.

SOMETHING . . . EXPLOSIVE HAPPENED HERE.

Interestingly, the universe is still exploding today, but it's not exploding as fast as it used to. According to Dr. Howard, most of it happened in the first second, which is why people call the beginning of the universe the "BIG BANG."

WHY NOT THE "BIG KABLOOIE"?

THAT'S NOT WORSE, ACTUALLY . . .

Dr. Howard says he's not a big fan of that name because technically the universe didn't "explode." According to him, space itself got big fast. But I think that just makes it cooler. I mean, who doesn't want to live in EXPLODING SPACE?

MOVIE IDEA:

EXPLODING SPACE! THE MOVIE!

STARRING:

DR. OLIVER!

IN WHICH SPACE EXPLODES!

I asked him how space itself can get bigger, and he said that in my story, instead of picturing all the kids running away from each other in the Narrows, I should imagine the hallway all of a sudden getting bigger:

That's basically what happened when the universe was born. It was all super-duper squished together, and then in one second, space exploded and got bigger, all the galaxies spread out, and the whole place got a lot emptier.

OK, I know what you're thinking at this point, which is: *That can't be how the universe started! What happened before that?* I totally get what you're thinking. How can the universe "start"? What was there *before* the Big Bang?

I thought of this question later at my house, so I texted Dr. Howard:

 HEY, DR. H.! QUESTION: IF THE UNIVERSE STARTED WITH THE BIG BANG, WHAT WAS THERE BEFORE??

HOW DID YOU GET THIS NUMBER?

 OH, MRS. HOWARD GAVE IT TO ME.

 SHE DID?

 YES, SHE SAID YOU COULD USE A HOBBY.

What Dr. Howard then said was pretty amazing. He said that nobody knows what happened before the Big Bang! That big explosion of space is as far back as we can see.

Dr. Howard said there are two theories or possible explanations:

THEORY #1: Time itself began with the Big Bang. This means that nothing happened before the Big Bang because there was no "before." It's like asking what a race was like before it started, and the answer is "nothing," because there was no race before!

NOT MY BEST RACE.

THEORY #2: There was another universe before the one we live in right now. Dr. Howard says that maybe our universe came from another universe getting crunched together, or maybe our universe was born *inside* of another universe.

IT'S A BABY UNIVERSE!

IT LOOKS LIKE YOUR MOTHER.

Nobody knows! And maybe nobody will ever know. It's like trying to remember what happened before you were born. You can't because you weren't born! (Although I'm guessing things were preeeetty dull before I came around.)

I had my own theory about where the universe came from:

WHAT IF OUR UNIVERSE IS ANOTHER UNIVERSE'S FART?

THAT IS A VALID THEORY, ACTUALLY.

Wherever it came from, it's pretty cool to think that our universe **HAD** a beginning. It makes it more relatable, you know? It wasn't always around, it used to be really small, now it's bigger, and it's still growing. Sound familiar?

IT'S JUST LIKE YOU AND ME!

CHAPTER 3
WATCH OUT FOR BLACK HOLES!

I had a fun summer vacation. That is, until I got stuck in my couch.

HELP!

Here is what happened: There were only two weeks of summer left before I started middle school. My parents wanted to go on a family road trip during the last week, which meant I really had only ONE week of vacation left.

MY LAST WEEK OF FREEDOM.

AUGUST

DO NOTHING
ROAD TRIP
SCHOOL START

Sure, I goofed around a lot these past few months, but this was my last chance to really do nothing, and I wanted to make it count. I even worked out a schedule. Granted, it was a pretty simple one:

Yes, my plan was to sit on the couch all week and just veg out. My dad is always trying to get me to do stuff, so he needed some convincing.

Of course, I wasn't actually planning on doing nothing. I had a list of important things to get done during my great couch sit-in:

COUCH TO-DO LIST:

- ☐ PLAY VIDEO GAMES
- ☐ READ BOOKS
- ☐ PLAY MORE VIDEO GAMES

A lot of people say they know how to veg out, but eventually they start doing something useful, like thinking about their chores or wishing they had done their chores earlier. I take my doing nothing pretty seriously.

LET'S DO THIS!

I had the perfect couch to do it in, too, because it's so old. My parents have had it since before I was born. They refuse to buy a new one until my sister and I turn eighteen because we're always spilling stuff and breaking things around the house.

So I sat down with my books and my video game console and got ready to start.

But then I realized, *What if I get hungry?* Doing nothing takes a surprising amount of energy, and I didn't want to have to get up again later. So I went to the kitchen to get some snacks and sat back down again.

NOW I'M
READY.

But then I thought, *What if I run out of books?*
Comic books are great, but they usually don't last
very long even if you reread them ten or twenty
times. So I went to get more books and sat down
one more time.

WHAT AM I
MISSING?

At this point, my spot on the couch was getting a little crowded, so when I realized I should also get my puzzle toys, my laptop, my tablet, and something to drink, it was a little hard to get off the couch.

Fortunately, that's when my sister, Veronica, happened to walk by.

OVER HERE!

Veronica is three years younger than me, and we get along pretty well. I've heard my mom tell other parents that we play nice together about 80 percent of the time. If you ask me, that's a solid B if they are giving grades for being siblings.

Unfortunately, today was one of the days during the 20 percent of the time when we don't get along, because when I asked her to bring me some of my stuff, she said she was "too busy."

I ended up having to bribe her. I told her I would give her a dollar for every item she brought me, which turned out to be both expensive and a bad idea. She took me up on my offer and brought me all the stuff I asked for and more: my Rubik's Cube, a gallon of milk, my archery set, my card collection, a baseball bat . . . She even brought me our dad's bowling ball!

She brought me so much stuff that I now owed her my next three weeks of allowance. Plus, I could almost feel my butt touching the floor from how much the couch cushions sank.

And that's how I got stuck in the couch. I started to think that maybe I would never get out, so I wrote my mom and dad a goodbye note telling them I was sorry for breaking Grandma's special vase. They probably hadn't noticed it's broken because I put it back together with chewing gum and gummy bears, but on a hot day it was going to be obvious.

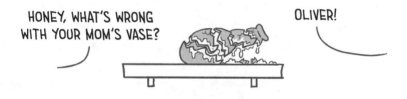

So what did my being stuck in a couch have to do with black holes? Well, being stuck in a couch is a lot like being stuck in a black hole.

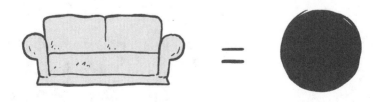

What are black holes? I'm glad you asked.

Black holes are these really cool things in space. Their name says it all: They're holes, and they are black. That sounds simple, but the thing about them is that instead of being holes ON something (like your old pants or a block of Swiss cheese), a black hole is a hole in **SPACE ITSELF.**

It's pretty strange to think of space having a hole, but that's what these things are. What's weird is that a regular hole only looks like a hole from above, so if you looked at a hole on the table from the side, it wouldn't look like a hole anymore.

REGULAR HOLE

But a black hole looks like a round hole no matter which way you're looking at it.

LOOKS LIKE A HOLE.

STILL LOOKS LIKE A HOLE.

LOOKS LIKE A HOLE.

Pretty weird, right?

Now, the reason they're called holes is that stuff can fall into them. Like if you throw a rock or your sister's bicycle into a black hole, it would fall in and . . . disappear. Poof. You'll never see that rock or bicycle again.

Another weird thing about them is that the more stuff you throw into them, the bigger the hole gets. That's how they work: You start with some stuff inside of them, and that stuff makes MORE stuff fall in, which makes the hole bigger, which makes *more* stuff fall in, which makes the hole even bigger, and so on, and so on . . .

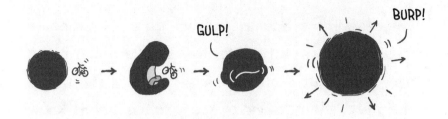

GULP!

BURP!

Dr. Howard says there are black holes all over the universe. A lot of them are in the center of galaxies, and they are super-duper big. For example, in the middle of the Milky Way there's a black hole that's about twenty-four million kilometers wide. The whole continent of Australia is only about four thousand kilometers wide, so this black hole is HUGE.

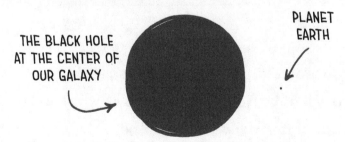

THE BLACK HOLE
AT THE CENTER OF
OUR GALAXY

PLANET
EARTH

(In case you're used to miles, a kilometer is a little more than half a mile.)

The reason Dr. Howard told me about black holes is that the week before, I was telling him I was nervous about starting middle school. The whole thing just seemed kind of scary to me. I don't know if you know this, but middle school isn't just a new school, it's a whole new **KIND** of school. They jam more kids in there than it's reasonable to do.

I HEARD IT GETS KINDA SMELLY.

WAIT UNTIL YOU GET TO HIGH SCHOOL.

Dr. Howard told me that middle school is kind of like a black hole. Nobody really knows what happens when you enter a black hole either. He said most likely you would get shredded to bits while you fall in and would probably never be able to get out. I told him this wasn't helping my nervousness.

But then he said that not knowing what's inside a black hole is actually one of the coolest things about them. He said scientists think that inside of black holes could be the answers to understanding how the universe really works.

He said some scientists even think that there could be whole other **UNIVERSES** inside of black holes. Each black hole could have its own universe inside of it with its own galaxies and stars, and maybe even its own people. In fact, **OUR** universe could be inside a black hole in **ANOTHER** universe. There could be a kid just like you in that universe looking at that black hole and wondering if **WE'RE** in it!

I think what **Dr. Howard** meant is that sometimes things can seem big and scary, but they can also be pretty exciting once you learn more about them. Like middle school: There probably wasn't going to be a whole new universe waiting for me, but maybe I would make new friends and learn some interesting things.

Anyway, back to my couch situation. Unfortunately, being stuck in the couch and thinking about black holes was a bad idea, because it also made me think about toilets.

One question you might have is, how can you see a black hole in space if space is ALSO black?!

CAN YOU SPOT THE BLACK HOLE?

SPACE

NOT EASY, RIGHT?

It turns out that black holes are also kind of like the toilet in your bathroom. You know how when you flush, all the water (and, er, other stuff) swirls around and around for a while before it goes down the hole in the middle? Well, the same thing happens with a black hole.

FLUSH!

The stuff that falls into a black hole, like asteroids, or gas, or your sister's bicycle, doesn't always fall straight in. It usually swirls around and around the black hole first.

And sometimes this swirly stuff is going so fast that it actually glows like a shooting star. This is what people sometimes see when they look at a black hole. For example, I found this picture online of a black hole that scientists took last year, and it totally looks like a giant, glowing toilet flush:

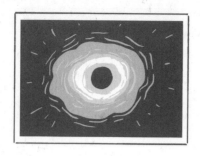

JUST GOOGLE "BLACK HOLE PHOTO."

And even if you don't see the glowing swirl of soon-to-be-flushed stuff, you can also tell where a black hole is by looking at how other stuff like stars swirl around the black hole. If you ever see some stars going in circles around an empty-looking spot in space, you can bet there's a black hole in the middle there.

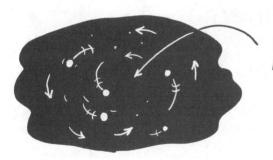

THERE'S PROBABLY
A BLACK HOLE THERE.

All this thinking about toilets made me realize there was a serious flaw in my plan to stay on the couch all week. I had to go to the bathroom.

I didn't think my sister would bring me a toilet no matter how much of my allowance I promised her. So I figured I should probably find a way to get out of there, or else my parents would REALLY have a reason to get a new couch.

That's when I remembered something else Dr. Howard told me. Dr. Howard said that most people think that if something falls into a black hole, it can never get out. That's because it's a hole in space, so no matter which direction you use to try to get out, you'll always stay in the hole. But he also said some scientists think there might be a LOOPHOLE.

A LOOPHOLE . . . IN A HOLE??

THIS THEORY IS FULL OF HOLES.

If you go all the way to the *center* of the black hole, some scientists think you could find a WORMHOLE, which is like a tunnel in space.

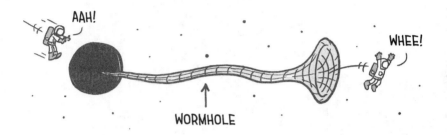

AAH!

WHEE!

WORMHOLE

That tunnel could end up taking you somewhere else in space, like maybe to another galaxy. If these tunnels exist, future astronauts could use them to go to other parts of the universe or talk to aliens that are really far away.

YOU'RE STARTING MIDDLE SCHOOL, TOO?

This gave me an idea. I wriggled to the bottom of the cushions and found a way out. It was just like a black hole, except instead of a wormhole, it was just a regular hole I could squeeze through. I told you this was an old couch.

I went to the bathroom, and while I was there, I had a question about black holes, so I video-called Dr. Howard.

"Hi, Dr. Howard!"

"Hi, Oliver. Wait, are you in the bathroom?"

"Yes, I am! Want to see my toilet flush?"

Then he hung up. So I called him again when I got out.

"Dr. Howard, I have a question about black holes."

"You're not still in the bathroom, are you?"

"No."

"Did you wash your hands?"

"Um . . . hold on . . . . . . OK. Yes, I did."

"What's your question?"

"How are black holes made?"

"That's actually a good question, Oliver."

"I know. I get all my best thinking done in the bathroom."

According to Dr. Howard, the recipe for making a black hole is pretty simple:

Step 1: Get some stuff (mountains, oceans, etc.).
Step 2: Squish it together a LOT until it's so squished it makes a hole in space.
Step 3: Run away really fast.

That's it. Dr. Howard says the hard part is squishing things enough to make a hole in space. For example, you can make a black hole out of planet Earth, but you'd have to squish the entire planet down to the size of a large marble. Imagine taking all the mountains, continents, oceans, trees, rocks, and lava on Earth and squashing it down to a little ball. That's pretty hard!

IF YOU SQUISHED THE ENTIRE EARTH INTO THIS CIRCLE, IT WOULD TURN INTO A BLACK HOLE.

Apparently, a lot of black holes get made when some stars in space explode, because the stuff inside the star gets squished so much that it makes a black hole. Dr. Howard told me some great stuff about exploding stars. More on that later.

The important thing is that I got out of the couch. And in case you are worried about falling into a real black hole, you can relax. They happen out there in space, really far away from us. But thinking about how you can make a black hole out of anything gave me a pretty good idea how I could get my allowance back from my sister . . .

CHAPTER 4
THE SQUISHPLODING SUN

Hey, I started middle school! Annnnddd . . .
I'm already in big trouble.

OLIVER!

Things started off well. Middle school is HUGE.
Students from all the different elementary schools
in town come together for middle school, so there
are a lot of kids I don't know. At drop-off, my dad
got a little emotional.

GOODBYE,
MY ONLY SON!

CHILL OUT, DAD.

Then we saw what eighth graders look like.

I guess kids change a lot between sixth and eighth grade:

If I'd known that's what I'm going to look like in two years, I might have stayed in elementary school.

Anyway, I got a locker, which is pretty sweet, and the cafeteria looks nice. I asked, and they don't serve potato tots, which is probably a good thing. All in all, it was a promising start to middle school.

I CAN DO THIS!

Then things took a turn for the worse in science class. Don't get me wrong, science class is cool. Out of all my classes, science is the one I most don't least look forward to, which means I actually look forward to it.

MY CLASSES	EMOJI RATING
SCIENCE	🙂
MATH	😐
ANCIENT HISTORY	🙂
SPANISH	😤
P.E.	😫
ENGLISH	😣

And the teacher is really nice. Ms. Valencia is the kind of person who can make even the weirdest science topic sound cheerful.

LET'S TALK ABOUT WHAT CAUSES FOOT FUNGUS!

But then I made a big mistake. As a get-to-know-you activity, Ms. Valencia asked us to write down the last interesting thing we remember learning about.

I was thinking this was my chance to impress her, so I wrote down everything I knew about gamma rays and how I was going to write a book that explains everything about the universe. I figure, if I'm going to be an astrophysicist, it can't hurt to get in good with the science teacher.

SHE'S GONNA LOVE THIS!

I thought she would read the answers when she got home, but when we finished passing them to the front, Ms. Valencia announced she was going to pick a few kids at random to read their answer in front of the whole class.

WHAT??

Well, I thought, *what are the chances she'll pick mine out of all these ki—*

"Oliver!"

She picked mine first.

I'm not usually afraid to talk in front of people, but these were all kids I'd never met before (remember, they came from different elementary schools). I did my best to warm up the crowd.

HEY, HOW ABOUT THAT HOT CALIFORNIA WEATHER, HUH?

BLANK STARES.

It was a tough audience. I took a deep breath and read my answer about gamma rays and the book I'm writing.

PRETTY COOL, HUH?

STILL BLANK STARES.

Then it got worse. Ms. Valencia got super excited about my book idea. She said she's never had a student do that before and asked if I would share the book with the whole class when I finish it.

WE CAN PRINT IT OUT FOR EVERYONE TO READ!

UH . . . SURE?

I mean, what else could I say? To be honest, I hadn't given much thought to the idea of anyone *actually* reading my book. I planned to write it, but knowing that a bunch of kids who I don't know are going to read it is a whole different thing. Suddenly, I felt a lot of PRESSURE.

The rest of the day went OK. Sven P. tried to impress the PE teacher with his armpit music, but he was so sweaty from playing kickball in class that his pits were out of tune.

And that was it. I had survived my first day of middle school. Except for the incident in science class, it was a pretty good day. All I had to do now was survive the walk home.

BEEEEEEP!
SCHOOL'S OUT!

HERE
WE GO . . .

For some reason, my teachers sent us home with the textbooks for all of our classes. I guess they do that so we can do our homework at home. Normally, getting books to take home is a good thing, but textbooks aren't exactly light reading material. When I got the first book, I went:

Then the second class handed out its textbook:

And the third . . .

By seventh period, I wasn't sure I could walk down the hall, much less all the way home.

It took three of us to stuff all the books into my backpack.

PUSH!

By the time school let out, the front exit looked like one of those nature shows where the baby turtles are trying to get to the ocean and you don't know which ones are going to make it or not.

HELP!

Not only was the backpack heavy, but it was SUPER HOT out. In California, it's still pretty warm in August. That day, it was hot enough to fry an egg on the cement.

As I was walking, I started to worry about having to finish my book about the universe for science class. I mean, I didn't even know what to write about next. Imagine trying to fill up a whole book! But then I looked up and realized the answer was staring me right in the face.

The SUN! I should tell you about the sun because the sun is pretty cool. Actually, it's super hot, which is the opposite of cool, but we'll get to that later.

THE SUN

It's pretty amazing to think about the sun because of how BIG it is. The sun is a giant ball of fire that's 1,400,000 kilometers wide. It's so big, you could fit one million planet Earths inside of it.

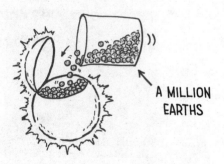

A MILLION
EARTHS

The only reason it looks so small in the sky is that it's really far away. The sun is 150 million kilometers away from Earth.

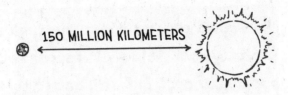

150 MILLION KILOMETERS

It's so far that if you tried to drive there, it would take you **150 years**. And if your dad drives as slow as mine, it will take you three hundred years.

HURRY UP, DAD!

Even light, which is the fastest thing in the universe, takes a while to get from the sun to here. Let's try a fun activity. First, close your eyes and imagine a ray of sunshine leaving the sun *right now*.

OK, now go look at a clock (on your kitchen wall or on your microwave) and wait.

Wait . . .
Wait . . .
Wait . . .

Has a minute passed? If so, then that ray of light is only one-eighth of the way to Earth!

ARE WE
THERE YET?

Wait some more . . .
Wait . . .
Wait . . .

Have four minutes passed? The ray of light is only halfway here!

I HAVE TO GO TO
THE BATHROOM.

Keep waiting . . .
Wait . . .
Wait . . .

Has it been eight minutes? If so, run outside and look up, because that ray of sunlight you imagined is only JUST NOW getting to Earth.

I'M HERE!

That means all the sunlight you ever see is actually eight minutes old. It spent eight minutes flying through space before it got here. You know when your mom asks you to do something and it takes her a while to figure out you actually got distracted and are doing something else?

OLIVER! WHERE'S THE LAUNDRY?

Well, something could happen to the sun, like it could turn purple, or explode, or disappear, and we wouldn't know about it for eight whole minutes!

POOF!

WHAT A NICE SUNNY DAY!

Now, remember when I said that the sun is a giant ball of fire? That's actually not true (sorry). Dr. Howard says the sun is not really burning, it's more like a nonstop **NUCLEAR EXPLOSION.**

THAT'S EVEN COOLER!

YOU REALLY LIKE EXPLOSIONS, DON'T YOU?

67

According to Dr. H., the sun is basically a big cloud of gas floating in space, and it all wants to squish together.

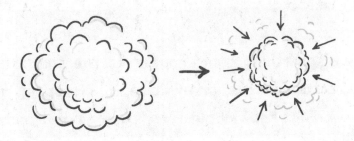

What happens is that the stuff in the center gets **EXTRA** squished because it's being squished by all the other stuff around it.

All that pressure in the middle is what makes the nuclear explosions. When the little bits of stuff get squished together so much, they smoosh together, which makes them explode.

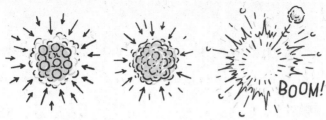

BOOM!

Normally, when things explode like that, they fly all over the place. But in the sun, the exploding stuff has nowhere to go because it's got all that other stuff around it trying to squish it in.

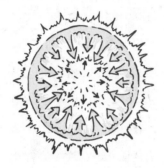

So the sun is squishing together **AND** exploding at the same time. It's that constant squishing and exploding that keeps it shining bright.

I told Dr. Howard I came up with a new name for what's happening inside the sun:

"SQUISHPLODING"!

THAT'S NOT BAD.

That's what the sun is: a giant, nuclear-powered, 1,400,000-kilometer ball of nonstop squish-ploding gas.

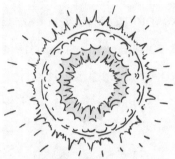

OK, remember when I said the sun is really hot? Well, the inside of the sun is a toasty 15,000,000 degrees Celsius, or 27,000,000 degrees Fahrenheit, which is super hot. It wasn't quite that hot on my walk home that day, but it definitely FELT like it was that hot.

IS IT 15 MILLION DEGREES HOT??

It didn't help that I kept seeing other kids getting a ride home from their parents.

It also didn't help that the sun was pushing down on me.

That's something else Dr. Howard told me. He said light can actually PUSH you. You don't feel it very much because it's only a tiiiiny bit, but it's there. He said light has energy, and when energy hits you, it pushes you a little. If you were in space and someone pointed a flashlight at you, you would start to move ever so slightly.

That's a cool fact, but it's the kind of thing that doesn't help when you're carrying a bunch of heavy books on a sunny day. Knowing that the sun is pushing you down even a little bit makes you wonder why there couldn't have been a few more clouds in the sky that day.

But I guess there are also good things that come from knowing this kind of stuff. For example, it made me realize that maybe feeling a little pressure to write my book isn't such a bad thing.

The center of the sun is also under pressure. If it wasn't, all that stuff inside would never do anything. The sun would just sit there and never shine. And without the sun, there wouldn't be any plants or animals or even people here on Earth!

THANK YOU, SUN!

Maybe having a little pressure to write my book will help. Without some pressure, I would probably just spend all my time playing video games and watching TV and not get any writing done.

I just hope my book shines and doesn't end up exploding like the sun.

Speaking of explosions, did you know the sun BURPS? It shouldn't be too surprising since it *is* full of gas. Sometimes the gas in the sun makes waves and bubbles that crash into each other, shooting a bunch of sun stuff out into space.

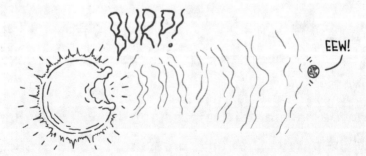

Dr. Howard says sometimes these burps (called "coronal mass ejections") are so big, they can make it all the way here to Earth. The sun stuff has electricity in it, so if it's an *extra* big burp, it can fry our computers and cell phones. Who knew solar indigestion could be so dangerous??

Also, did you know the sun is growing? Right now, it's growing bigger and bigger every day, and one day it might grow so much that Earth will be INSIDE the sun (burned to a crisp).

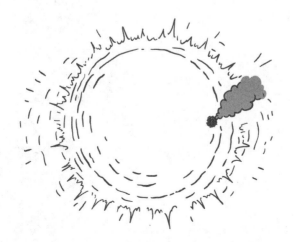

But then at some point, the sun is going to run out of stuff to squish together and the nuclear explosions will stop. Then the sun is going to shrink and just simmer there like when my little sister gets mad at me if I get extra screen time.

GRRR . . .

But don't worry, all of that is not going to happen for billions of years. Until then, the sun is going to keep on shining brightly.

Finally, I made it home! It felt like I was still millions of kilometers away, but when I looked up, I was in front of my house.

My sister was outside watering the plants with the hose, so I asked her for a drink of water. She had the hose on "shower" mode and ended up soaking me.

I didn't mind, though. It felt pretty good.

But then I remembered . . .

AH!
MY BOOKS!

My books got soaked, too! They were ruined! It looks like I'm going to have to carry more of them home again.

CHAPTER 5
THE EIGHT PLANETS AND, UM, PLUTO

Well, it finally happened. I got sent to the principal's office in middle school, and it's not looking good.

YOU'RE IN A LOT OF TROUBLE, MR. OLIVER.

I'll tell you all about how I got here, but first I should tell you the good news: I made a new friend!

EXTRA! EXTRA! READ ALL ABOUT IT!

OLIVER MAKES A FRIEND!

At first, I was nervous about making friends in middle school, so I kind of overdid it. I told everyone I met that I'm writing a cool book about the universe and tried to show them the pages I had written. Most kids looked at me funny.

But there was one kid who liked the idea. Her name is Evie, and we became friends pretty quick.

Evie is great. One time she walked home with me, and we played video games all afternoon. Since it was her first time, I let her win.

(If she tells you that she beat me and I got really frustrated, **DON'T BELIEVE HER.**)

One day, we were having lunch in the cafeteria. It was spaghetti and meatballs day, which is good. Spaghetti and meatballs is one of the best things they serve, especially when they put a slice of cheesy bread on top.

Evie started to eat her lunch, but something about one of my meatballs caught my attention.

It reminded me of Mercury, one of the planets in our solar system (that's the group of planets that goes around our sun).

First of all, this meatball is round and it's warm. Mercury is also round and warm. It's the closest planet to the sun, so it stays nice and toasty. And there's no air or water on Mercury, so it looks like a lumpy gray-brown ball, just like this meatball.

MEATBALL   (SEE THE RESEMBLANCE?)   MERCURY

Mercury is cool because it's the fastest planet in the solar system. It's going so fast, it only takes three months for it to go all the way around the sun, whereas Earth takes twelve months.

A "year" is what we call the time it takes a planet to go around the sun, which means that a year on Mercury is much shorter than here. If you lived on Mercury, you would celebrate your birthday every three months!

Evie thought that was super interesting. And then she had an awesome idea. She thought we should make comics about the planets for my book. Evie is a really good artist. She can draw pretty much anything you ask her to.

One time I asked her to draw a shark fighting a dinosaur, and it looked totally professional.

She thought we should make the comics about the planets as if they were middle school students, which I thought was hilarious. There are eight planets in total, and they are (in order of closest to farthest from the sun): Mercury, Venus, Earth, Mars, Jupiter, Saturn, Uranus, and Neptune.

We made a plan to draw a comic every day at lunch break. Drawing these comics is what got us in trouble with the principal, but more on that later. First, you have to read the comics, because they're pretty funny.

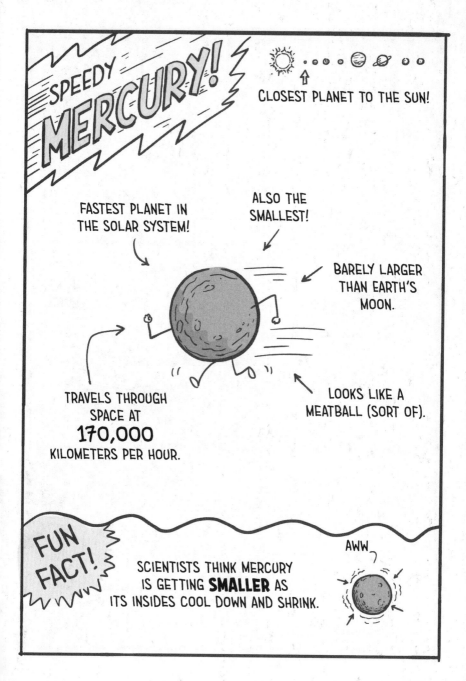

SPEEDY **MERCURY!**

CLOSEST PLANET TO THE SUN!

FASTEST PLANET IN THE SOLAR SYSTEM!

ALSO THE SMALLEST!

BARELY LARGER THAN EARTH'S MOON.

TRAVELS THROUGH SPACE AT **170,000** KILOMETERS PER HOUR.

LOOKS LIKE A MEATBALL (SORT OF).

FUN FACT!

SCIENTISTS THINK MERCURY IS GETTING **SMALLER** AS ITS INSIDES COOL DOWN AND SHRINK.

AWW

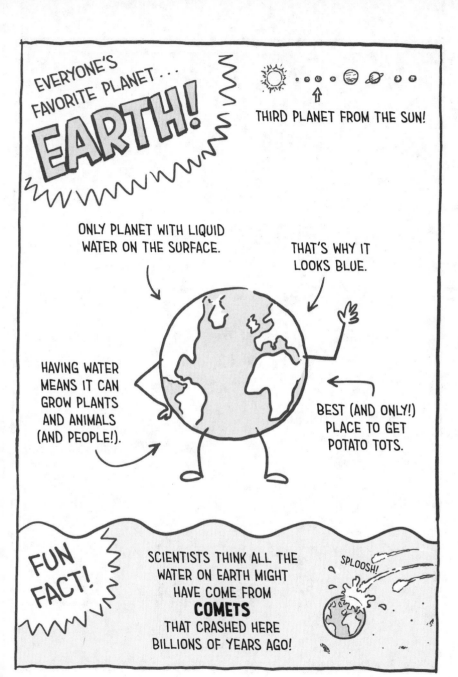

EVERYONE'S FAVORITE PLANET...

EARTH!

THIRD PLANET FROM THE SUN!

ONLY PLANET WITH LIQUID WATER ON THE SURFACE.

THAT'S WHY IT LOOKS BLUE.

HAVING WATER MEANS IT CAN GROW PLANTS AND ANIMALS (AND PEOPLE!).

BEST (AND ONLY!) PLACE TO GET POTATO TOTS.

FUN FACT!

SCIENTISTS THINK ALL THE WATER ON EARTH MIGHT HAVE COME FROM **COMETS** THAT CRASHED HERE BILLIONS OF YEARS AGO!

SPLOOSH!

THE SAD STORY OF PLUTO

FOR A LONG TIME,
PEOPLE THOUGHT PLUTO
WAS A PLANET . . .

BUT THEN SCIENTISTS
REALIZED . . .

IT'S ACTUALLY SMALLER
THAN OUR MOON!

SO THEY DECIDED IT WAS
TOO SMALL TO BE CALLED
A PLANET.

THE MOON   PLUTO

STILL, THE OTHER PLANETS LET PLUTO HANG OUT.

WE STILL
LIKE YOU.

GEE, THANKS!

These are the first comics we made. We decided to make Earth the main character because Earth is like an average kid. It's true, Earth is pretty average, and that's what makes it special. It's not the biggest or the smallest planet in the solar system, and it's not the hottest or the coldest.

It's just in the right place for there to be liquid water on it, which you need to grow plants and animals (and people). If Earth was hotter, all the water would boil off, and if it was colder, it would all freeze.

The next day, we drew some comics about Venus and Mars.

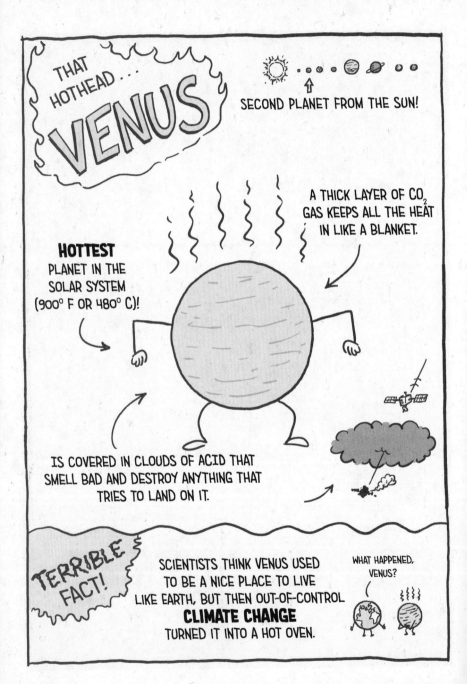

THAT HOTHEAD...

VENUS

SECOND PLANET FROM THE SUN!

A THICK LAYER OF CO_2 GAS KEEPS ALL THE HEAT IN LIKE A BLANKET.

HOTTEST PLANET IN THE SOLAR SYSTEM (900° F OR 480° C)!

IS COVERED IN CLOUDS OF ACID THAT SMELL BAD AND DESTROY ANYTHING THAT TRIES TO LAND ON IT.

TERRIBLE FACT!

SCIENTISTS THINK VENUS USED TO BE A NICE PLACE TO LIVE LIKE EARTH, BUT THEN OUT-OF-CONTROL **CLIMATE CHANGE** TURNED IT INTO A HOT OVEN.

WHAT HAPPENED, VENUS?

MYSTERIOUS MARS!

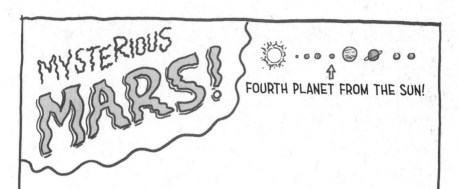

FOURTH PLANET FROM THE SUN!

MARS HAS WATER, BUT IT'S ALL FROZEN OR HIDDEN UNDER THE GROUND.

IF YOU MELT ALL THE ICE AT THE TOP AND BOTTOM OF MARS, IT WOULD MAKE ENOUGH WATER TO COVER THE WHOLE PLANET.

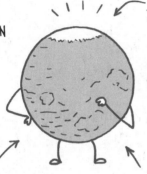

MORE THAN 12 ROBOTS FROM EARTH HAVE LANDED ON MARS.

MARS LOOKS RED BECAUSE IT'S FULL OF RUST FROM ALL THE IRON IN THE ROCKS.

FUN IDEA!

IT'S POSSIBLE THAT LIFE ON EARTH ACTUALLY CAME FROM MARS, AND THAT IT CAME TO EARTH ON AN ASTEROID.

WHEE!

93

Venus and Mars are the closest planets to Earth. Together with Mercury and Earth, they're the planets that are made mostly out of rocks (the others are mostly gas and ice). I like to think that when nobody is looking, they form a rock band together. Get it? A ROCK band?

At this point, our comics started to get popular. A couple of kids came over, and they thought the few we made were pretty good.

So we kept going with Jupiter and Saturn.

THE BIG GUY...

JUPITER!

FIFTH PLANET
FROM THE SUN!

BIGGEST
PLANET IN
THE SOLAR
SYSTEM.

NO ONE MESSES
WITH JUPITER.

MOSTLY MADE
OF GAS WITH A
FUZZY ROCKY
CENTER.

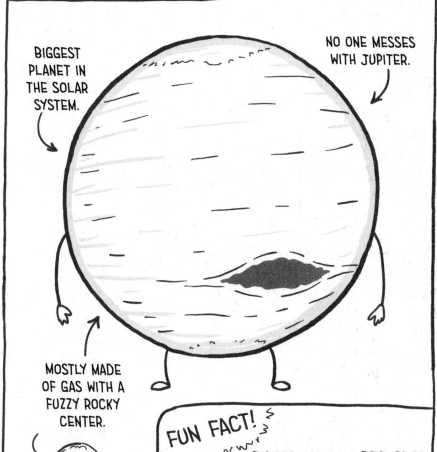

FUN FACT!

JUPITER HAS A BIG **RED SPOT**
THAT'S ACTUALLY A STORM YOU
CAN SEE FROM SPACE.

The Bling Queen Saturn

SIXTH PLANET FROM THE SUN!

LIKE JUPITER, IT'S MOSTLY MADE OF GAS.

SECOND-LARGEST PLANET IN THE SOLAR SYSTEM.

SATURN'S RINGS ARE MOSTLY MADE OF ICE BITS THAT ORBIT AROUND THE PLANET.

SATURN ALSO HAS THE GREATEST NUMBER OF MOONS (82)!

BLING FACT!

SCIENTISTS WHO STUDY SATURN THINK THAT IT RAINS **DIAMONDS** THERE INSTEAD OF WATER!

One thing that's hard to tell sometimes in books is how big the planets are. If you were to line them all up for a family photo, this is what it would look like:

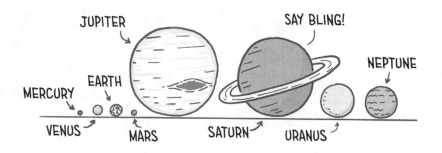

Our comics were getting even more readers. When we finished the Jupiter and Saturn comics, we even had kids we didn't know come over to read them.

And that's when we got in trouble.

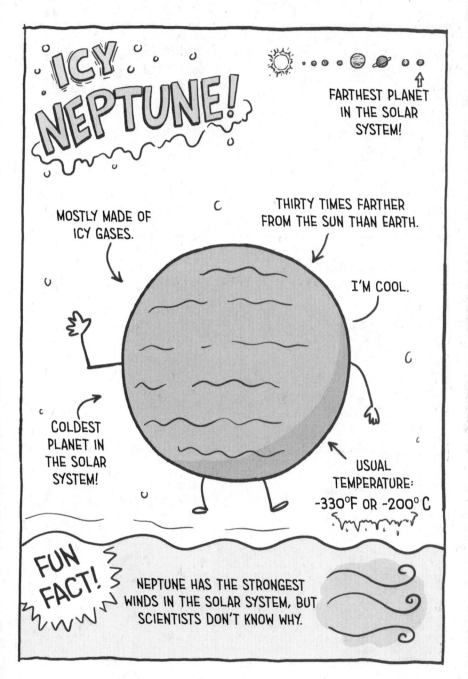

ICY NEPTUNE!

FARTHEST PLANET IN THE SOLAR SYSTEM!

MOSTLY MADE OF ICY GASES.

THIRTY TIMES FARTHER FROM THE SUN THAN EARTH.

I'M COOL.

COLDEST PLANET IN THE SOLAR SYSTEM!

USUAL TEMPERATURE: -330°F OR -200°C

FUN FACT!

NEPTUNE HAS THE STRONGEST WINDS IN THE SOLAR SYSTEM, BUT SCIENTISTS DON'T KNOW WHY.

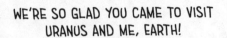

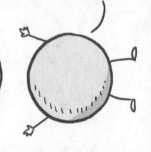

FUN FACTS ABOUT

URANUS!

↑ SEVENTH PLANET IN THE SOLAR SYSTEM!

☐ **URANUS IS BIG!**
IT'S THE THIRD-LARGEST PLANET IN THE SOLAR SYSTEM.

☐ **URANUS IS COLD!**
COLDER THAN ANTARCTICA!

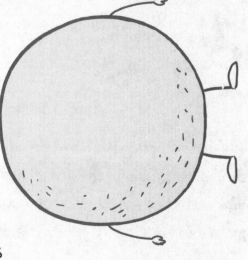

☐ **URANUS STINKS!**
IT HAS CLOUDS OF THE SAME GAS THAT MAKES FARTS SMELL BAD.

☐ **URANUS IS TILTED!**
IT'S THE ONLY PLANET THAT SPINS SIDEWAYS.

Uranus and Neptune are the last planets, and they are WAY out there in the middle of nowhere. Their orbits (the round-like paths planets take when they go around the sun) are HUGE.

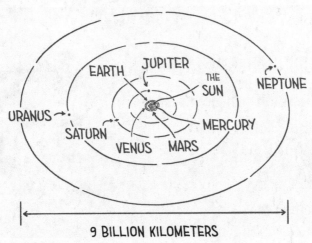

9 BILLION KILOMETERS

Kids at the cafeteria REALLY seemed to like these comics, especially the last two pages. We got a huge crowd at lunch, and they couldn't stop laughing. We were instant celebrities!

HA-HA! SO FUNNY!

Evie and I were very excited coming back from lunch.

But then later in homeroom, Mr. Lee, the assistant principal, came into the classroom and pointed at me. I'd been called enough times in elementary school to know what that meant: I was in **TROUBLE**.

Outside the classroom, I saw that Evie was also being taken out of her homeroom.

I asked Mr. Lee what was going on, and he said they were looking for the kids who were making comics in the cafeteria earlier today.

UM . . .

DO YOU KNOW WHO IT WAS?

Uh-oh, were we not supposed to draw comics in the cafeteria? Did we make too much of a commotion? Right away, I had a flashback to fourth grade and my ex-friend, José.

FLASHBACK SQUIGGLE LINES

One time in fourth grade I got into trouble because I accidentally flushed a sandwich down the toilet in the school bathroom. By "accidentally," I mean

I did it on purpose because I was curious to see what would happen. What was accidental was what happened next, which sort of became school legend.

Unfortunately, my friend José was with me at the time, and he got in trouble, too, by association. After that, his grandma advised him to not hang out with me, so we stopped being friends.

I learned an important lesson that day. When you get in trouble, sometimes you get your friends in trouble, too, and they might stop being your friends. Also, if you're going to flush something down the toilet, you should break it up into little pieces first.

So when Mr. Lee asked who had made the comics, I raised my hand and said it was all me so Evie wouldn't get in trouble.

Mr. Lee seemed skeptical, so he asked me to draw something to prove it. I did my best to draw him a bunny rabbit.

He still wasn't convinced, but when I told him it was all my fault anyway, he signaled to the other teacher to let Evie go back to her homeroom. Then he took me to the principal's office.

GULP.

Ms. Rajagopalan, the middle school principal, said she heard a lot about me from Dr. Narro, my last principal. I calmly gave her my explanation of the situation.

I'M SORRY, I DIDN'T KNOW YOU COULDN'T DRAW COMICS IN THE CAFETERIA!!

She said of course I could draw comics in the cafeteria. The reason she called me into her office was what the comics were about.

OK, now I was confused. What could be so bad about talking about the planets?

Then Ms. Rajagopalan seemed confused. She said she'd heard I was making comics about, ahem, BUTTS.

And then it hit me. This was all because of Uranus. You see, when some people see the word "Uranus," they read it as "ur-A-nus," which sounds like you're talking about your butt. But actually, the right way to read it is "URah-nus."

IT'S JUST MISPRONOUNCED!

I explained this to Ms. Rajagopalan, but she was still a little suspicious. She said I could have done it on purpose to hide making a comic about butts. So I decided to call in an expert witness. I asked Ms. Rajagopalan if I could borrow her phone, and I called Dr. Howard.

I CALL DR. HOWARD TO THE STAND!

RIIIIING . . .

This is how it went:

Dr. H.: Hello, who is this?

Me: Dr. Howard, do you swear to tell the truth, the whole truth, and nothing but the truth?

Dr. H.: I should have known it was you, Oliver.

Me: I'm in the principal's office, and you're my expert witness, Dr. H.

Dr. H.: If I hang up, you're just going to keep calling, aren't you?

Me: Why wouldn't I?

Dr. H.: [*Sigh.*] What's your question?

I told Dr. H. what was going on, and he confirmed to Ms. Rajagopalan everything that was in the comic.

He said Uranus (pronounced "URah-nus") really IS on its side. All the other planets spin in place kind of like a top as they go around the sun, but Uranus spins more like a screwdriver or a football.

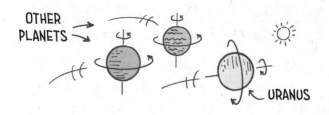

OTHER PLANETS

URANUS

Scientists think a giant asteroid hit Uranus billions of years ago, and that's how it ended up spinning that way.

OWW!

Dr. Howard then said that spinning on its side makes the days on Uranus really wacky. For example, if you lived in the north pole of Uranus, a day would last EIGHTY-FOUR YEARS! He offered to give us a whole presentation about it with slides and everything, but that's when Ms. Rajagopalan cut him off.

I COULD SHOW YOU SOME GRAPHS—

THANK YOU, DR. HOWARD.

Ms. Rajagopalan said that since the science I wrote is all true, then I could keep making the comics. But she asked me to always put instructions on them to tell kids how to pronounce URANUS properly so there's no butt confusion. I asked if I absolutely HAD to do that.

And that's when she kicked me out of her office. When I told Evie I didn't get in trouble, she was really glad.

She said I shouldn't have taken all the blame, though. I told her I'd be sure to give her credit in my book and that we should draw one last comic about the planets. And here it is:

115

CHAPTER 6
SPOOKY SPACE STUFF

There's something SPOOKY going on around here.

I'm all alone in my house and I'm totally freaking out. Why? Because I just heard something upstairs, and I think it's a *ghost*. And it doesn't help that it's the scariest night of the year:

My Halloween started off pretty well this morning. This year Halloween is on a Friday, so the school let us come to class dressed up in our costumes. Evie came dressed as her favorite Japanese animation character. I'd never heard of it, but apparently a lot of kids had, which made her really popular.

Her costume was really elaborate. Me? I didn't remember I needed a costume until last night. I had to think creatively, so I came up with a brilliant idea. I grabbed my ninja costume from last year and stuffed it with a pillow and a couple of couch cushions.

Nobody got it. I was a black hole! What could be scarier than a mysterious object from space that sucks stuff in and traps it inside forever? I had to walk around all day hearing everyone get it wrong.

Clearly, more people need to learn about all the amazing stuff that's out there in space. I told everyone that's the reason I was going to stay home and work on my book instead of going trick-or-treating. Evie was bummed.

I tried to pass it off like I didn't like candy. And then later, when my mom asked me why I wasn't going trick-or-treating, I told her I was getting too old for it.

The truth is I **LOVE** candy. I mean, how can you not? It's sweet and delicious. And walking around getting a bucketful of it for free from neighbors is something I would happily do even when I'm really old.

But the thing is, trick-or-treating sort of creeps me out. My neighborhood goes all out with the Halloween decorations, and they make the street look really spooky. Last year, I was out trick-or-treating, and I was already feeling a little freaked out when one of my neighbors jumped out wearing a super-realistic Wolfman costume!

So this year, I'm just going to stay home and work on my book. Don't worry, though, I still have a plan to get candy. I told my sister I'd give her a quarter for every piece of candy she brought back for me, except she said I still owed her money from that time I was stuck in the couch.

I had to offer to fold her half of the family clothes the next time Mom does laundry (that's one of our chores), and she said she'd trade that for a

quarter of her candy loot. I think that's a *sweet*
deal (get it?).

BRING BACK
THE GOOD
STUFF!

Anyway, my whole plan to have a scare-free Halloween kind of didn't work out, because when my
parents left to take my sister trick-or-treating,
I was left at home all by myself, and now I'm convinced that my house is **HAUNTED**. That's right,
haunted as in **GHOSTS**.

GULP.

It started after everyone had left. I settled in to
start typing, and then I felt it. I had the spooky
feeling I wasn't alone in the house.

I always knew my house was a little cursed. There are always weird things happening, like that time I was playing Monopoly with my sister and I landed on one of her properties FIVE TIMES IN A ROW. That kind of thing doesn't happen by coincidence.

THIS GAME IS POSSESSED!

UH-HUH.

Or that time I couldn't find my history assignment even though I looked for it all over the house. I eventually found it at the bottom of my book bag, but I bet it was a ghost that put it there.

OH, HERE
IT IS.

I decided to start a video meeting with Dr. Howard to get his help. I figured if anyone knows anything about ghosts, it's someone who studies the universe for a living. Ghosts are part of the universe, aren't they?

Here's how it went:

OLIVER

"Dr. Howard, HELP! There's a ghost in my house!"

DR. HOWARD

"Hi, Oliver. Is this a Halloween prank?"

"No, it's for real! I'm home alone and I think there's a ghost here with me."

"Interesting."

Usually, when Dr. Howard says "interesting," it's because someone has asked him a question he's never heard before. I guess this is the first time anyone has asked him about ghosts.

"So you're all by yourself," Dr. H. said, "it's dark, and even though you can't see it, you can feel there's something there."

"Yup," I said.

"Well, the good news is that I don't think it's a ghost."

"Really? Phew!"

Then he said:

"But it could be GHOSTLY PARTICLES."

Dr. H. says there's something in the universe called **NEUTRINOS.** I know, the name makes it sound like a crunchy snack or a brand of frozen mini hot dogs, but Dr. H. says they really exist and that they're a lot like ghosts.

Imagine tiny bits of stuff that are there, but you can't see them and you can barely feel them. Dr. H.

says neutrinos are like that because they don't feel the same forces that we do. For example, they don't stick to or push against atoms the same way we do, and light doesn't bounce off them. They mostly only feel a force called the **WEAK FORCE**, which, as you can probably guess, is pretty weak.

Because of that, neutrinos just kind of pass through you as if you weren't there, kind of like a ghost would.

He said billions of them are made in the center of the sun, and they just fly right through Earth like it was made out of nothing.

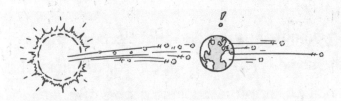

I asked Dr. H. if the ghost in my house could be a bunch of neutrinos, and he said, "Maybe."

Because neutrinos feel the weak force, you can sometimes tell if a lot of neutrinos are passing through you. Every once in a while, a tiny neutrino might bump into one of your atoms using the weak force, and if it does, you might be able to feel it.

He told me to sit really still and see if I could feel anything.

"Are you sitting still?" he asked.

"Yup."

"Do you feel anything?"

"Yes. My butt itches."

"I don't think that's a neutrino."

"Hold on, let me scratch. Ahhh . . . OK, now I'm sitting still."

After a while, I told him I couldn't feel anything.

"Hmm, then it's probably not neutrinos," he said.

"Phew!"

"But it could be DARK MATTER."

HUH??

Dr. Howard says there's ANOTHER kind of spooky stuff in the universe called DARK MATTER, and this one is super-extra mysterious. He said dark matter is all around us, and like neutrinos, it's also invisible (light doesn't bounce off it) and you can't touch it (it doesn't feel the same forces that push and pull stuff that we do).

CREEPY!

In fact, dark matter is *extra* invisible, because scientists don't think it even feels the weak force. This means it's almost impossible to tell if there's a bunch of it going through you at any moment.

I'M INVISIBLE!

I know what you're thinking. If we can't see or touch this stuff, how do we even know it's there? Dr. H.

said that dark matter does feel one thing: gravity. Gravity is what makes things clump together in space. It's also what makes you fall to the ground when you jump up or when you trip. When you fall to the ground, that's actually you clumping together with the earth because of gravity.

Dark matter feels gravity, so scientists can tell where it is in space by seeing how galaxies clump together. If there's a galaxy that's clumping more than it should, you can bet there's a whole bunch of invisible dark matter keeping it together.

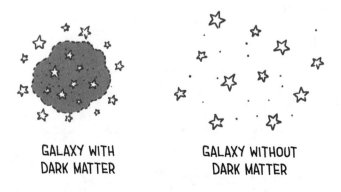

GALAXY WITH
DARK MATTER

GALAXY WITHOUT
DARK MATTER

It's kind of like how you can tell someone has brought a new game or gadget to school. If you see a bunch of kids clumped together before class starts, there must be something fun there.

I asked Dr. Howard if the ghost in my house could be dark matter, and he said, "Maybe."

"Does the gravity in your house feel different?" he asked.

"I do feel heavier," I said.

"You do?"

"Yeah, but it's probably because I ate a whole pepperoni pizza for dinner."

"That's not what I meant."

"I ate so much I think I'm going to make a lot of dark matter in the bathroom tomorrow, if you know what I mean."

"Unfortunately, I do know what you mean."

I looked around the room, and it didn't seem like the gravity was any different. I told Dr. Howard nothing was clumping together or looking extra heavy or floating around. That would be pretty spooky.

"Hmm . . ." said Dr. Howard. "That means it's probably not dark matter."

"Phew!"

"But it could be DARK ENERGY."

WOW!

There's MORE spooky stuff in the universe?! Dr. Howard said dark energy is the ultimate spooky stuff in the universe. He said it's not even stuff, it's just pure, invisible energy. And it's so powerful it's making the universe EXPLODE.

Remember when I told you that the universe started with an explosion and that it was still exploding today? Well, dark energy is what keeps that explosion going. It's an invisible energy that's PUSHING everything apart. Scientists have no idea what it is or what's making it, so they gave it the mysterious-sounding name of dark energy.

WHY NOT "WEIRD ENERGY" OR "PUSHY ENERGY"?

THOSE ARE GOOD, TOO.

Dr. H. says dark energy isn't just pushing everything apart, it's making space BIGGER. It's stretching space so there's more and more of it all the time. If the universe was a balloon being inflated, dark energy is like the pump that's making the balloon stretch and grow.

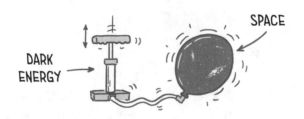

I told Dr. H. I had no idea there was so much spooky stuff in the universe, and he said that just because something is spooky doesn't mean you have to be afraid of it. For example, if it wasn't for dark matter, a lot of galaxies wouldn't clump together at all. Maybe without dark matter the Milky Way wouldn't have formed, and then we wouldn't be here!

And if it wasn't for dark energy, the universe could stop exploding and gravity might clump it all back into a tiny little dot again. That would be bad news, because then we'd all be crushed.

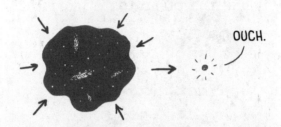

OUCH.

Even neutrinos are useful, because since they're made inside of stars, they can tell us a lot about how suns work. A lot of neutrinos are made when stars explode, too, so they can tell us when the explosion happened and how big of an explosion it was.

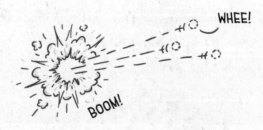

WHEE!

BOOM!

I guess that's pretty cool. But I still had a question for Dr. Howard.

"What about the ghost in my house?!"

. . .

"Hello?"

DR. HOWARD??

That's when our video meeting got cut off. Suddenly, I heard a big noise from upstairs.

AAHH!

CLUMP!

I don't know if it's neutrinos, dark matter, or dark energy, but whatever is in the house is *moving*. I can hear it taking steps down the hallway on the second floor.

Now it's coming down the stairs! Aaaahhh! If this is the last thing I write, please tell my sister to bury me with my share of the candy loot.

It's getting closer! I can feel it right behind me!

It's . . .
It's . . .

It was my dad.

It turns out my dad had stayed behind and was taking a nap upstairs the whole time. It wasn't dark matter or dark energy I was sensing in the house.

It was just Dad matter.

I THOUGHT YOU WERE A GHOST!

I THOUGHT YOU WERE!

I called Dr. Howard back and told him what happened, and he said he had a hunch I wasn't really alone in the house. He thinks it's funny that my dad thought *I* was a ghost. Dr. H. says that's also how the universe is. There's actually more of the spooky stuff (dark matter and dark energy) in the universe than there is the regular kind of stuff that you and I are made of. If the universe was a cake, this is what it would look like:

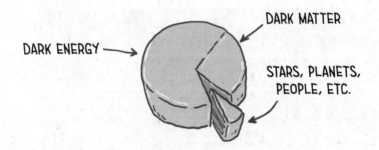

DARK MATTER

DARK ENERGY

STARS, PLANETS, PEOPLE, ETC.

About a quarter of the cake would be dark matter, and two-thirds would be dark energy. That means almost **95** percent of the universe is invisible spooky stuff. Only a thin slice (about **5** percent) would be all the stars and galaxies and planets and people in the universe. To the universe, WE'RE the weird, spooky stuff!

After I hung up with Dr. Howard, I heard a knock on the door. It was Evie and Sven.

I wasn't sure if I should go, but then I decided to brave it. It's a spooky universe, but I guess it's less spooky with friends.

People still couldn't tell what my costume was, though.

NICE HAIRBALL COSTUME.

I'M A BLACK HOLE!

CHAPTER 7
A GINORMOUS UNIVERSE

Have you ever had something go so wrong it turns into a big disaster? Well, that's what happened to me in art class. Except, it wasn't just a big disaster, it was a UNIVERSE-SIZE disaster.

I probably should have known that something bad was going to happen because I'm not much of an artist. Don't get me wrong, I can draw a pretty epic space-battle scene with dragons and everything. It's good as long as you don't mind that everyone is a stick figure, and the dragons look more like cats with long noses.

I think I used to draw a lot more as a little kid, but then my parents said one time I took a permanent marker and drew all over the house. Lots of kids do that, but in my case "all over the house" included my baby sister and her clothes.

I don't remember what I drew on her, but I'm sure it was an improvement. I don't think Mom and Dad agreed, though, because after that it was really hard to find a marker anywhere in the house. In other words, I blame my parents for the fact that I never got beyond stick figures.

It wasn't even my idea to join the art class. Evie thought it'd be fun if we were all in it together, so Sven and I signed up for it with her. The surprising thing is that it wasn't even about drawing.

Ms. Swan (that's the art teacher) says you can make art by doing anything, not just drawing. In fact, she said there are no rules in art. I asked her if that meant we could just take a nap or play video games in class. She said there are no rules in art, but art CLASS still has a few rules.

Then she gave us our assignment, which was to sculpt something out of clay. She said we could sculpt whatever we wanted because she had a ton of clay in a wheelbarrow, and that got everyone excited. Mateo S., who is a super-artist, said he was going to sculpt a scene from his favorite opera by someone called Verdi. No one was really surprised.

Evie said she was going to make a sculpture of her pet hamster, Siggy. I told her that should be pretty easy because Siggy just looks like a little ball of fur that sits around and sleeps all day, but she didn't think that was funny.

Even Sven knew what he wanted to do. He likes to play tennis, so he decided to sculpt a tennis racket. Me? I had no idea. I asked Ms. Swan what I should do, and she said I should think about what inspires me.

But then I had a better idea: I should make a sculpture of the universe. I mean, I've been writing so much about the universe for this book, I bet I could make a sculpture of it with my eyes closed. Plus, nobody else was trying to make something as awesome as the universe, so I figured I'd get points for being original.

Unfortunately, that's where the trouble began.

My first step was to get some clay for my sculpture. But to do that, I had to figure out how MUCH clay to get. And that made me think about how BIG the universe is.

THE UNIVERSE

I asked Dr. Howard this question once, and he said this would be a good topic to talk about in my book. He said knowing how big the universe is would really help kids today get some perspective and appreciation for the context in which etc., etc. (Insert adult lecture here. I kind of stopped paying attention.)

I do remember what he said afterward, though, mostly because I like the word "bajillions." You see, you have to use that word a lot when talking about the size of the universe. It's SO BIG.

Let's start with how big Earth is. Earth is about forty thousand kilometers wide. That sounds like a lot, but it's pretty small compared to the sun, which is 1,400,000 kilometers wide. If you were to draw the two of them next to each other, this is what they would look like:

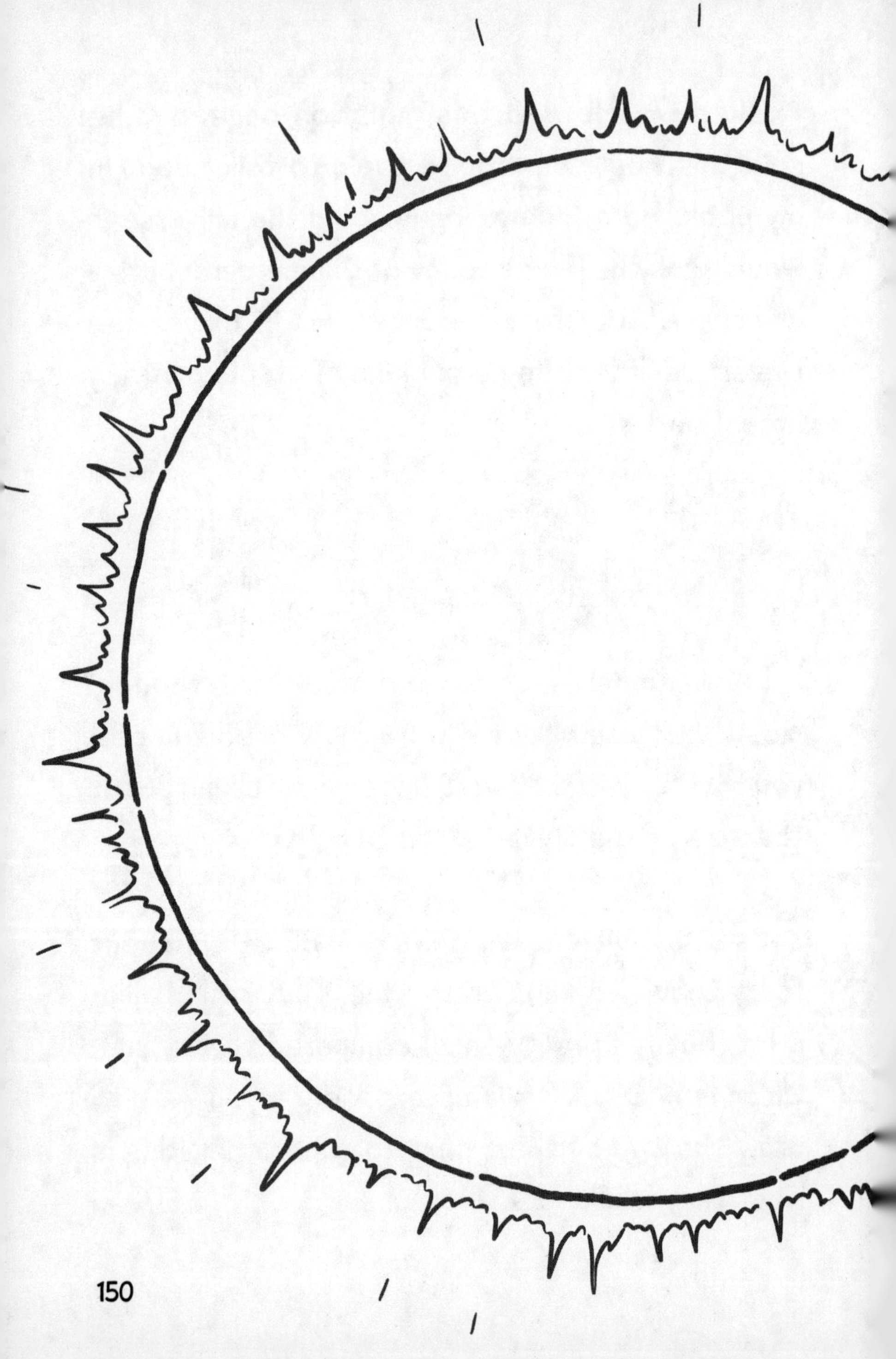

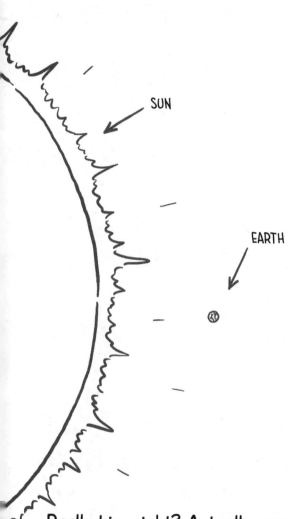

SUN

EARTH

Really big, right? Actually, our sun isn't even the biggest star around. There are stars out there that are *thousands* of times bigger than our sun.

For example, there's one called **UY Scuti** that's 2,300,000,000 kilometers wide. Next to the sun, it looks like this:

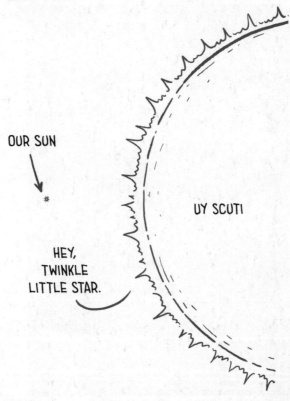

OUR SUN

UY SCUTI

HEY,
TWINKLE
LITTLE STAR.

I know, UY Scuti sounds like the name of a cartoon, but who am I to argue with something that big? Can you imagine what it would be like to be next to it? You'd have to move a lot if it ever asked you to "Scuti" over.

GET IT? INSTEAD OF "SCOOT"?

I GET IT.

Dr. Howard says that at some point, the numbers for the size of things in space start to get a little ridiculous. Our sun, for example, sits in a swirly galaxy full of stars called the Milky Way. The Milky Way is about 1,000,000,000,000,000,000 kilometers wide. That has so many zeros it makes your eyes glaze over.

THE MILKY WAY

THE SUN

IS THAT A BAJILLION??

IT'S A QUINTILLION.

1,000,000,000,000,000,000 KM

The Milky Way is so big, it takes light a hundred thousand years to go from one end to the other. Light is the fastest thing in the universe, so that's saying a lot. Light is so fast it can go around Earth seven and a half times in one second. Now imagine going as fast as light and STILL having to wait a hundred thousand years to go from one side of the galaxy to the other. That's how big the Milky Way is.

I NEED TO GO TO THE BATHROOM.

Dr. Howard says the Milky Way is just one galaxy in a huge group of galaxies called the Laniakea Supercluster. This supercluster has about a hundred thousand galaxies in it and is about 5,000,000,000,000,000,000,000 kilometers wide.

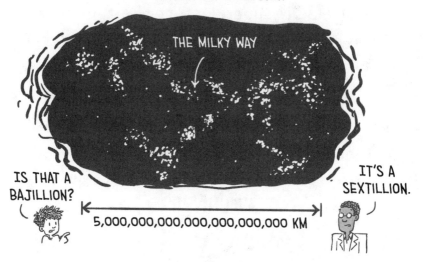

THE LANIAKEA SUPERCLUSTER

THE MILKY WAY

IS THAT A BAJILLION?

IT'S A SEXTILLION.

5,000,000,000,000,000,000,000 KM

At this point my head was spinning. We're teeny-tiny compared to Earth, and Earth is teeny-teeny-tiny compared to the sun. But then the sun is teeny-teeny-teeny-tiny compared to the Milky Way, and the Milky Way is super-duper teeny-tiny compared to the Laniakea Supercluster. Is that where the universe ends?? Nope.

I NEED TO LIE DOWN.

WELCOME TO MY JOB.

Dr. Howard says there might be as many as **TEN MILLION** superclusters like the Laniakea Supercluster in the universe. That's over two trillion galaxies. I asked Dr. H. how big that makes the universe, and he said that as far as we can see, the universe is 900,000,000,000,000,000,000,000 kilometers wide.

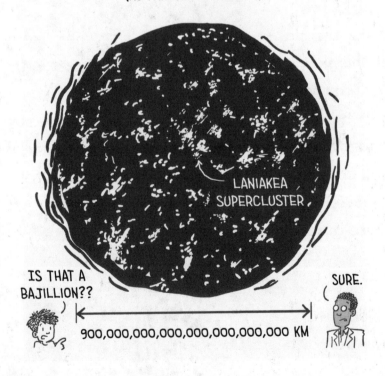

THE UNIVERSE
(AS FAR AS WE CAN SEE)

LANIAKEA SUPERCLUSTER

IS THAT A BAJILLION??

SURE.

900,000,000,000,000,000,000,000 KM

Clearly, I was going to need a LOT of clay. If my sculpture was going to represent the universe, I needed to make it as big as I could. So I asked Ms. Swan if I could have extra clay.

I took the clay to my table, and it seemed like a lot. I looked over at Evie, and suddenly, making a small hamster seemed like a better idea.

You might have noticed that Dr. Howard said the universe was as big as "as far as we can see." That means it could actually be bigger. I asked him why we couldn't see the whole universe, and he said it's just too big. There are parts of the universe that are so far away that the light from there still hasn't gotten to us.

Dr. H. calls the stuff around us the OBSERVABLE UNIVERSE because it's the part of the universe that our eyes and telescopes can see. It's like being out in a field in the middle of the night with a tiny flashlight. The flashlight can show you only the things that are close to you, so you're kind of in a bubble where you have no idea how big the field actually is.

It could be that the field you're in is huge, or it could be that it ends right outside the bubble of light. In the same way, the universe could be 900,000,000,000,000,000,000,000 kilometers wide, which is as far as we can see, or it could be much bigger than that.

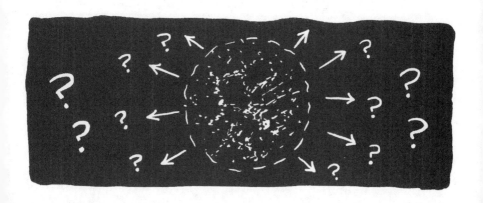

Just in case, I decided to get more clay. Ms. Swan had stepped out of the classroom, so I helped myself. I figured she would support me being more scientifically accurate in my art, and I used the wheelbarrow to bring the rest of the clay to my table.

Evie looked a little worried, but I told her this was nothing compared to how big the universe could be. Dr. H. says it's possible that the universe is actually INFINITE. That means it goes on and on in all directions FOREVER.

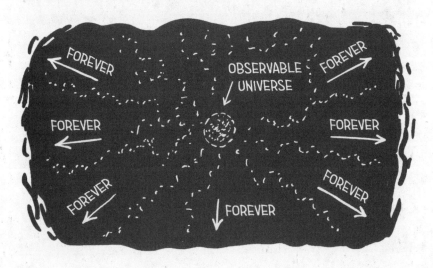

That would be pretty amazing, because it wouldn't just mean that space goes on forever. It might mean there's an infinite number of stars and an infinite number of planets. And there might be an infinite number of planets with things living on them. In other words, there could be an infinite number of **ALIENS** out there!

Dr. Howard says the other possibility is that the universe is **FINITE**, which means it doesn't go on forever. This possibility was better for me, because Ms. Swan didn't have an infinite amount of clay. Also, making an infinite sculpture would take a really long time and, well, lunch was next period. I wasn't ready to make that kind of sacrifice for art.

My next problem was that I didn't know what shape to make my sculpture. It was supposed to be shaped like the universe, but . . . what shape is the universe?

Dr. Howard says it's really hard to tell what the shape of the universe is because we can't see all of it. We can see only a part of it (remember the observable universe?).

But scientists have done some measurements out in space, and they have some ideas about what the shape of the universe could be. These ideas are:

POSSIBILITY #1: THE INFINITE MEATBALL

Dr. Howard says that if the universe is infinite, it probably looks like a giant meatball. He didn't really say the word "meatball," he said "a big sphere," but I was hungry at the time, and I called it a meatball.

He said if the universe is infinite, you can imagine our view of the universe growing and growing like a giant sphere ~~meatball~~ that gets bigger and bigger forever.

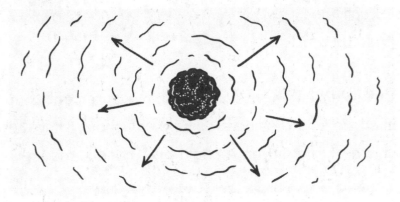

POSSIBILITY #2: THE COSMIC BURRITO

Another possibility is that the universe is shaped like a really long burrito. Dr. Howard used the word "cylinder," but something long and circular sounded a lot like a burrito to me (I told you I was hungry).

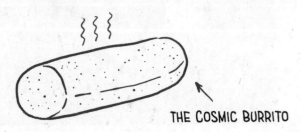

THE COSMIC BURRITO

He said a shape like this means that the universe is infinite on one side. If you go along the long side of the burrito, you could keep going forever. But if you went in the rolled-up direction, you would actually go in a circle and end up in the same place you started!

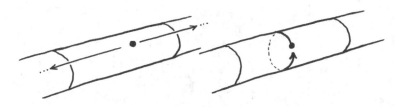

POSSIBILITY #3: THE MAGIC DONUT

The last possibility is that the universe is shaped like a donut. I guess I was already thinking of dessert. Dr. H. says the technical term is a "torus," but scientists call it a donut, too.

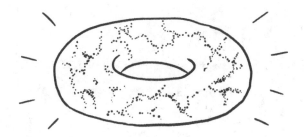

He said a donut would be a cool shape for the universe because it would mean it was finite (it wouldn't go on forever in any direction). It would also mean that no matter which way you went, you'd always come back to the same place. It's true, look:

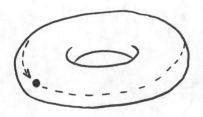 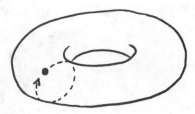

If you go around the outer edge of the donut, you make a big circle and come back to the same place . . .

. . . and if you go into the hole, you make a small circle and ALSO come back to the same spot.

In space, that would mean that if you got on a spaceship and flew in one direction for a long time, you would eventually get to the same place from the *other* direction.

Anyway, that's how I ended up with a giant donut on my sculpting table.

TA-DA!

I picked the donut out of all the possible shapes of the universe because it seemed like the most fun. I mean, wouldn't it be amazing to live inside a donut? It definitely sounds better than living inside a meatball or a burrito.

NOW I'M HUNGRY!

I told Dr. Howard later what I did, and he said I didn't have to choose one shape or the other. He said some scientists think there isn't just **ONE** universe. There could be **LOTS** of universes out there. One possibility is that each of those universes is a different shape. There could be a universe shaped like a donut, and another like a burrito, and another like a donut burrito, etc.

DONUT

BURRITO

DONUT BURRITO?

This idea is called the multi-verse (as in "multiple universes"), and it's pretty mind-blowing. I mean, you think there's only one universe, and then you find out there could be MORE of them?

Here I kind of wish I *was* in one of those other universes, because this is when the disaster happened. Remember when I told you that I had a universe-size disaster? Well, it turned out that the tables we were using for our sculptures weren't meant to have an entire universe of clay sitting on them. It started with a crack.

UH-OH.

Suddenly, the table leg broke, sending my donut universe rolling toward the other sculptures!

I tried to warn everyone, but it was too late.

Poor Siggy didn't stand a chance.

Sven's racket? It was point, set, and match.

And Mateo? You know how they say, "It ain't over 'til the opera lady sings"? Well, she sang.

In the end, it was a universe-size disaster. A donut-shaped universe-size disaster.

I felt terrible! I tried to apologize.

And that's when Ms. Swan came back into the classroom.

I wasn't sure what to say, so I just blurted out:

Then her reaction surprised everyone.

She thought it was really clever of us to work together to make a sculpture of the universe with all kinds of things in it. She said opera singers, hamsters, and rackets are all part of the universe, after all. She was so impressed with it that she gave us all special little art medals and extra credit.

I guess it's true what Dr. Howard said. It does help to have the right perspective about the universe. What seems like a disaster can sometimes turn into something awesome if you think about the BIG picture.

That's when class ended and we headed to the cafeteria, which was a good thing. All this talk about universe-size food had given me a universe-size appetite.

Uh-oh, I'm running out of time.

You would think that an eleven-year-old kid like me would have all the time in the world, but between school, homework, chores, karate class, piano lessons, and reading comic books and playing video games, I barely have any time left.

HAVE YOU DONE YOUR CHORES?

I STILL HAVE 0.25 MINUTES OF SCREEN TIME LEFT!

And now I have a deadline for writing my book. Ms. Valencia (my science teacher) says I can present it in class whenever I want. But if I want to have any hope of finishing it, it has to be before the holiday break. This is because of something Dr. Howard told me when I went to visit him. I was curious to see where he worked, so my mom took me to his university office.

"Hi, Dr. H.!"

"Oh, you're early."

"So, this is your office, huh?"

"Yes."

"I thought it'd be bigger."

"How can I help you, Oliver?"

I had some questions for him about the universe, and he gave me some awesome answers, but then at the end he dropped a bombshell on me.

OK, he's not *leaving* leaving. He said he's moving away for a year to go work on a new giant telescope being built in India. His whole family is going, and they'll be in a totally different time zone, which means it's going to be hard for me to call him to ask questions.

The point is that if I want to finish this book, I need to do it now before he leaves next month. That doesn't give me a lot of time, especially after I learned **ANOTHER** big bombshell. I'll tell you about that one at the end of the chapter.

SPOILER ALERT:
IT'S A
MAJOR
PLOT TWIST.

So, let's get to it. In this chapter, I've decided to tell you something I've been spending a lot of time thinking about: TIME! That's right, it's time to take the time to talk about time (and the universe).

Remember I told you my family went on a road trip at the end of last summer before classes started? We went to see my cousins, and that was fine (I'll tell you about that another time), but *getting* there was SUPER boring.

SIGH.

We had to spend hours in the car with nothing to do. Of course, it didn't help that my little sister kept trying to cross the invisible line between our two halves of the back seat.

HEY, YOU'RE ON MY SIDE!!

AM NOT!

It also didn't help that she had her tablet and I couldn't get to mine or my video game console because my dad had buried them deep in the trunk of the car. All I could do was sit there and stare out the window. It. Was. SO. Boring. It felt like time was moving sssuuuuuppppppeeeeerrr ssslllllloooooooowwwwww. Every time I asked my parents how long we'd been in the car, it was like no time had passed at all!

ARE WE THERE YET?

NOT YET, OLIVER . . .

HOW ABOUT NOW?

YOU ASKED TEN SECONDS AGO!!

I had to stop doing that because my dad said if I asked "Are we there yet?" one more time, he'd pull over and leave me on the side of the road. I was tempted to see if he would do it, but I didn't want to give my little sister the satisfaction of getting the whole back seat to herself.

I was so bored I started doing something I almost never do, which is to sit there and think. I thought about the weird cactuses we passed by and about this one cloud in the sky that looked like a giant fluffy butt.

Then I started to wonder if it WAS possible for time to be moving slower for me. It definitely *felt* like it. So when my sister fell asleep, I grabbed her tablet and called Dr. Howard. Here's how it went:

"Aah! Who is this?"

"Hi, Dr. H. It's me, Oliver."

"Why do you look like a giant bunny rabbit?"

"Oh. That's my sister's camera filter. Sorry, I don't know how to turn it off.

"Oh, wait, I can change it to a giant emoji. Is that better?"

"Not really. What's your question?"

I explained to Dr. Howard my theory that time was moving slower on my car ride, and, to my surprise, he said I was right!

NO WAY!  WAY!

Dr. Howard explained that something super weird and cool about the universe is that time doesn't always move the same way everywhere. He said there are places in space where time is moving slower, and there are places in space where time is moving faster.

NO WAY!  WAY!

It's really weird, because you'd think that time would be the same everywhere, but Dr. H. says that's not how the universe works. He said there are two things that can make time move slower for you:

1) If you're close to something big and heavy and
2) If you're going really fast.

The first one is pretty mind-blowing. It means that if you are close to a black hole (which is big and heavy from all the stuff squished inside of it), then to someone far away, you're going to look like you're moving in slow motion.

HHHHHEEEELLLLOOO . . .
HHHHOOOWWW AAARRRREEE
YYYOOOU..?

And it doesn't just happen with black holes. It also happens here on Earth:

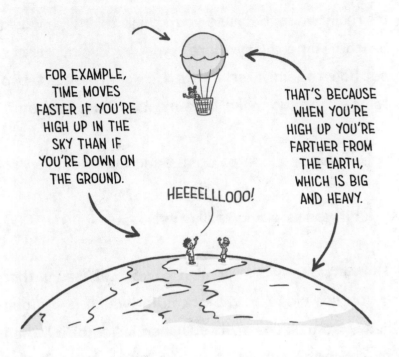

FOR EXAMPLE, TIME MOVES FASTER IF YOU'RE HIGH UP IN THE SKY THAN IF YOU'RE DOWN ON THE GROUND.

THAT'S BECAUSE WHEN YOU'RE HIGH UP YOU'RE FARTHER FROM THE EARTH, WHICH IS BIG AND HEAVY.

HEEEELLLOOO!

Dr. Howard said it happens only a little on Earth because Earth is not as big and heavy as a black hole. But still, it happens. Scientists have done experiments where they put clocks on hot-air balloons or airplanes, or high up on mountains, and they compare them to clocks that stay on the ground. After a while, the scientists can tell the clocks that are high up run faster a tiny little bit, like a few nanoseconds every few hours.

It's pretty cool to think that time moves differently for different things here on Earth. If you went down into the ground, you would be even closer to the earth. Dr. H. says that the center of the earth is younger than the rest of the earth by a few years because it's about as close as you can get to the whole planet, so time moves slower there.

WHAT CAN I SAY? I'M YOUNG INSIDE.

And it also means your FEET are moving slower in time than the rest of you. When you stand up, your feet are closer to the earth than your head, so time moves slower for them.

I asked Dr. Howard if the same was true for little sisters. Since they are closer to the ground, is that why they're so slow?

The other thing that can make time move slower is pretty amazing, too. Dr. Howard said time moves slower when you're moving really fast. This is why he said I was right about my car ride theory. The car is moving, so everything inside of it is moving slower in time.

I'MMMM SSSOOOO BBBBOOOORRRREEDD . . .

He said anything that moves is also moving slower in time, but you wouldn't really notice it unless you were going **REALLY** fast, like almost as fast as the speed of light. The speed of light is the opposite of how fast my dad drives, so Dr. H. doesn't think time slowed down very much for me in the car.

CAN'T YOU GO FASTER?

I'M DRIVING AT A SAFE SPEED!!

He said that if you *were* to go super fast, then some really weird things could happen. I was still super bored in the car, so I decided to write it as a comic. It's an epic space adventure called *Epic Space Adventure!* Are you ready? Here it is:

ONE DAY, EPIC SPACE ADVENTURER OLIVER DECIDED TO FLY TO ANOTHER PLANET . . .

← EPIC SPACE BASE

SO HE HOPPED ON HIS AWESOME SPACESHIP . . .
THE *EPIC* SPACESHIP.

EPIC

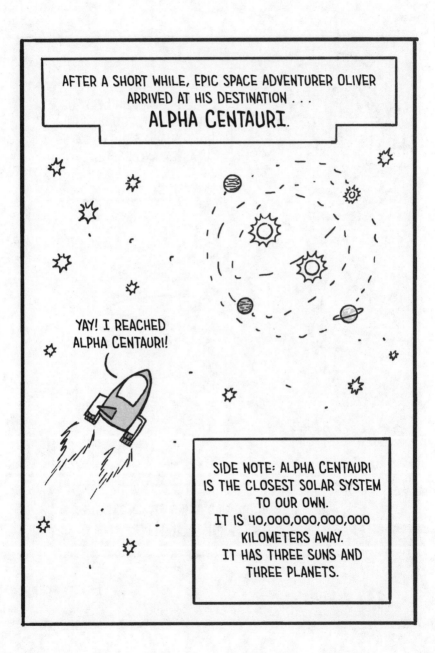

HE FLEW BACK TO EARTH AT ALMOST THE SPEED OF LIGHT AGAIN . . .

BUT WHEN HE LANDED BACK ON EARTH, HE HAD A **BIG SURPRISE** WAITING FOR HIM . . .

Pretty good plot twist, huh? You can probably figure out what happened. The whole time space adventurer Oliver was in the spaceship going super fast, time was moving really slow for him. But for his sister, who stayed behind, time kept going normally, and she got older.

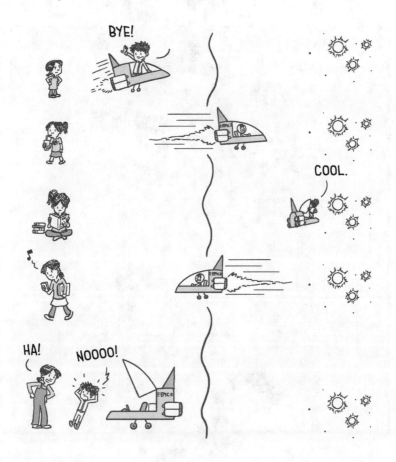

The whole trip actually took nine years (that's how far Alpha Centauri is from Earth), but because space adventurer Oliver was stuck in slow motion, he hardly noticed any time had passed at all!

Dr. Howard says scientists don't really know why this slowing down of time, either by being close to something big and heavy or by going really fast, happens. It just does. He said it's one of the weirdest things about the universe. Well, he said that and having a conversation with a kid with an emoji face.

CHECK THIS ONE OUT!

Speaking of time, my dad may not have been driving very fast, but by the time I finished writing my epic space adventure in the car, we arrived at my cousins' house. I guess even if you're not going at the speed of light, sitting and thinking about stuff can help time go by faster, too.

And speaking of shocking plot twists, I have to tell you the other big bombshell I learned this week. You might have noticed that my epic space adventure has really good art. That's because they're not my drawings. They're Evie's. She walked home with me after school the other day and redrew the whole thing.

Evie and I have become pretty good friends these last few months. Even though we went to different elementary schools, it's like we've known each other for a long time. We play video games, talk about manga and comics, and have pretty funny conversations about cats and our siblings.

The big bombshell came when her dad picked her up from my house. She usually walks home after hanging out, but today for the first time one of her parents came to get her. I went to open the door and had one of the biggest shocks of my life.

DR. HOWARD!?

OLIVER!?

Dr. Howard is Evie's dad!!!

I guess I never mentioned Dr. Howard to Evie, and I never thought to ask what Evie's full name is (it's Evelyn Layla Howard). We all had a pretty good laugh about it. Since Evie and I are friends, this means I can go over to Dr. Howard's house anytime to ask him questions. Dr. Howard didn't seem as excited as I was about that.

I was feeling good about it, but then as they were walking away, I realized what the *really* big plot twist was.

WAIT A MINUTE . . .

If Dr. Howard was leaving at the end of the month, that meant Evie was leaving, too!

Well, that's it. It's all over.

My entire middle school future
is coming to an end, and it's all
because of a hamster named Siggy.

SIGGY

You probably remember Siggy from my universe-size disaster. He's Evie's hamster, which she made a sculpture of in art class. You know, the one she thought was super cute? She even printed a T-shirt with him on it.

SO CUTE!

The first thing you should know about Siggy is that he's not Evie's hamster anymore. He is my hamster. After I found out that Evie was leaving to go with her family to India for a year, Evie said she had something important to ask me.

YOU CAN SAY NO, BUT . . . WILL YOU TAKE CARE OF SIGGY FOR ME?

She can't take Siggy with her, so she asked me to look after him. I'm not a big fan of tiny furballs, but Evie said it would mean a lot to her. Plus, she said she would call all the time to talk to Siggy, and I figured the furball would be a good excuse for us to keep in touch.

OK.

YES!

Evie dropped him off a week before she was supposed to leave so I could get used to taking care of him, and she showed me the basics.

REMEMBER TO ALWAYS CLOSE THE LID!

The second thing you should know about Siggy is that he's actually not my hamster anymore either. That's because he's no longer with us. I took really good care of him, I promise! For the first couple of days, I fed him, changed his water, cleaned up after him . . . I even started to bond with the little guy.

HUH. HE IS KIND OF CUTE.

But then one morning I went to clean his plastic box, and I realized I had left the lid a little open. When I looked inside, Siggy was gone!

He must have climbed up and escaped! I looked everywhere for him. Did he climb up to a window and jump out? Did he run past me and sneak out the front door? All I knew was that he was nowhere to be found.

I felt so bad! What was Evie going to say? I was NOT looking forward to having to tell her. And the worst part is that all of this happened the day I was supposed to present my book to Ms. Valencia's science class. When I was walking to school that morning, I kind of wished the universe would end so I wouldn't have to do either of those things.

On my way to school, I decided to text Dr. Howard.

"Hi, Dr. Howard."

"Good morning, Oliver. How's Siggy?"

"Uh, yeah . . . About that . . . What are the chances the universe will end in the next twenty minutes?"

"Pretty much zero."

"Aww."

I asked Dr. Howard if it was even possible for the universe to end, and he said it wasn't likely.

"Most scientists think the universe is going to go on forever," he said.

"I see."

"BUT . . ."

"But?"

"But some really weird things might happen to it."

HOW WEIRD?

According to Dr. H., there are three things that might happen to the universe, and it all depends on, well, farts. Remember I told you that the universe began like a bunch of kids stuck in a hallway, and then all of a sudden someone farted?

Well, what happens to the universe next sort of depends on what that fart does. Remember I also told you that the universe is still exploding today? That explosion is basically powered by that fart. If you remember, scientists call it dark energy.

The first possibility is that the fart just hangs around and spreads. That means the kids are going to keep running away in all directions.

Eventually, the kids will run so much, they'll be super far away from each other.

And then they'll be super bored.

That's kind of what's going to happen to the universe if dark energy just hangs around forever.

The universe is going to keep getting bigger and bigger, and all the things in it are going to get farther and farther apart from each other until it all gets super boring.

WHERE DID EVERYBODY GO?

Scientists call this the "heat death of the universe," but I think a better name for it is the "Big Blah." Dr. H. seemed to agree.

"Yeah, 'blah' is a good way to describe a cosmic state of maximum entropy or blandness," he said.

"I know, right? They should put me in charge of naming things in science."

I CAN BE THE "NAMER-IN-CHIEF"

Dr. H. told me the other two things that can happen to the universe, but I'll tell you about those in a minute. Of the three, the Big Blah was exactly how I was feeling when I got to school. I wasn't ready to tell Evie what happened, so I kind of avoided her.

Sven found me, though. When I told him I had lost Siggy, he agreed that Evie was going to be super bummed out. But he said he sympathized with me. He used to have a pet snake, and when he lost it at home, his parents were **NOT** happy.

HERE, LITTLE
COBRA . . .

It wasn't very hard to hide from Evie right before first period. Things get pretty crowded in the morning rush at school. In fact, it's a lot like the second thing that might happen to the universe. Dr. H. said the second possibility is that dark energy (which is what's making the universe explode) could just . . . go away. It's like if the fart that was making all the kids run away suddenly disappeared.

Then the kids wouldn't have any reason to keep running away, and eventually they would turn around and start coming together again.

Pretty soon they'd be right back where they started, with everyone clumped together.

I STILL WANT MY POTATO TOTS . . .

In space, the clumping together would be done by gravity. Gravity could pull all the stars and galaxies in the universe together and scrunch them down into a tiny little dot again, maybe forever.

SCRUNCH!

Dr. H. said scientists call this possibility the "Big Crunch," which is totally what I would have called it, so . . . good job scientists!

[OLIVER APPROVED!]

Back in school, I managed to avoid Evie almost to the start of first period. I didn't have a class with her, but my first class was science, which meant it was time to do my book presentation. I was almost inside the classroom when suddenly, Ms. Valencia saw me.

I did my best to stay hidden, but Ms. Valencia was blowing my cover.

I decided to duck down with the excuse of getting my book.

YEAH, I HAVE IT RIGHT HERE!

And that's when I **FELT** it.

There was something small and furry in between my books. It was . . .

SIGGY!!

He had gotten into my backpack and had been hiding there the whole time! Somehow, he managed to not get squished. I had never been so glad to see a little furball in my life. I would have given him a hug, except we were still at school and I didn't want to be known as a hamster hugger. Ms. Valencia was a little surprised.

IS THAT . . .
A HAMSTER?

I think Siggy was surprised by Ms. Valencia, too, because that's when he jumped out of my hands. You know how in movies, when something really dramatic happens, things start to move in super-slow motion? Well, that's exactly how Siggy leaping out of my hands felt for me.

N-N-N-N-0-0-0-0 . . . !!

To make matters worse, Siggy ran off into the huge crowd of kids walking to their classes.

SIGGY!!

I didn't know what to do! I thought about shouting, "HAMSTER ON THE LOOSE!!" but I didn't want to create a panic. In a flash, it reminded me of the third weird thing that Dr. Howard said can happen to the universe. Dr. H. said it's also possible for dark energy to get MORE powerful in the future, which would *rip* the universe apart. Imagine if the fart in the hallway suddenly got stronger and stinkier as it spread. It would cause total chaos! Kids would start running like crazy and tripping all over each other.

Dr. Howard says scientists call this the "Big Rip" because the universe would get bigger so fast that galaxies and stars and planets would get ripped and shredded to bits.

It's . . . not a good picture. And that's what I wanted to avoid at school. The only problem was that it wasn't up to me anymore. Some kids started noticing Siggy running around on the floor.

I tried to run after Siggy before it got any worse, but I couldn't get through the crowd. What if someone accidentally squished Siggy??

Then I heard a scream.

It was Evie!

She got everyone to stop, and Siggy ran right up to her.

Yeah, I had a lot of explaining to do. But Evie wasn't mad. She was just happy Siggy was OK.

After that, Ms. Valencia said Siggy could stay in her classroom for the rest of the day. He even became kind of a celebrity among all the kids, the little furball.

You might be wondering what happened to my book presentation. I told Ms. Valencia that the book wasn't finished yet, that I still had to write one more chapter, and that it was going to be about the end of the universe. That's the chapter you're reading now. Ms. Valencia said that I could show it once I was done writing.

So, to recap: The universe is probably not going to end, but some weird things might happen to it. It might keep getting bigger, or it might scrunch together, or it might get ripped apart. It all depends on what dark energy (also known as the big hallway fart) ends up doing.

YEAH, I'M A STINKER.

DARK ENERGY

But you don't have to worry. Dr. Howard says that if the universe does get crunched or ripped, it's not going to happen for billions and billions of years. And he says scientists have been doing measurements of space and they don't think it's going to happen anyway. The universe is probably just going to keep on growing and getting more boring, which is totally fine with me. I think I've had enough excitement for a while.

CHAPTER 10
THE END OF THE BOOK

A few days later, I presented my book in class. I was nervous, but I think everyone liked it. Some of the kids came up to me afterward and asked if they could read it.

SURE!

I told them I would have to print more copies for them because I only had one and it was for someone else. After school that day, my dad took me over to give it to them. Luckily, I caught them just as they were about to leave for the airport.

Dr. Howard said he looked forward to reading it and asked if this meant I was going to stop calling him. I told him that now that I'm an expert on the universe, he could call ME if he had any questions.

HA! I WILL!

Evie was excited to see her drawings in the book. She said we should work on another one while she's in India.

WE COULD MAKE IT ALL ABOUT HAMSTERS!

UH . . .

I told her I'd think about it.

But we'll definitely keep in touch. It's not like she was going into a black hole or anything.

And that's it! I hope you enjoyed the book. It turns out that I *am* good at something, which is talking about farts. I'm sure there's something you're really good at, too, and if you haven't found it already, I bet you will. It's a pretty big universe, after all.

EPIC SPACE ADVENTURER OLIVER WAS SUPER BORED BECAUSE HIS BEST FRIEND, EVIE, HAD JUST MOVED AWAY.

I'M SO BORED!

THEN HE HAD AN **AWESOME IDEA:**

I KNOW! I'LL GO LOOK FOR ALIENS AND MAKE NEW FRIENDS!

EVEN THOUGH HIS (NOW OLDER) SISTER TOLD HIM HE HAD TO CLEAN HIS ROOM, OLIVER JUMPED INTO HIS SPACESHIP AND TOOK OFF!

HEY!

BYE!

HE TRAVELED AT ALMOST THE SPEED OF LIGHT . . .

I CAN'T WAIT TO MAKE ALIEN FRIENDS!

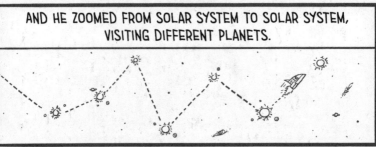

AND HE ZOOMED FROM SOLAR SYSTEM TO SOLAR SYSTEM, VISITING DIFFERENT PLANETS.

SOME OF THE PLANETS WERE TOO CLOSE TO THEIR STAR, SO THEY WERE TOO HOT TO HAVE ALIENS.

YOW!

AND SOME OF THEM WERE TOO FAR FROM THEIR STAR, SO THEY WERE TOO COLD.

BRR!

SOME WERE IN THE RIGHT PLACE BUT MISSING THINGS LIKE WATER AND AIR.

GASP!

HE STARTED TO GET TIRED, SO HE CHECKED HOW MANY PLANETS HE STILL HAD TO VISIT.

HE LEARNED THAT EACH GALAXY USUALLY HAS ABOUT 100 BILLION STARS AND ABOUT 100 BILLION PLANETS! (SOME STARS HAVE LOTS OF PLANETS, OTHERS HAVE NONE.)

GALAXY

100 BILLION STARS
100 BILLION PLANETS

AND THERE ARE ABOUT 100 BILLION GALAXIES IN THE OBSERVABLE UNIVERSE, WHICH MEANS HE STILL HAD ABOUT 10,000,000,000,000,000,000,000 PLANETS LEFT TO VISIT!

WHAT!?

SO HE GAVE UP AND WENT BACK HOME, ZOOMING AT ALMOST THE SPEED OF LIGHT AGAIN!

I'M GETTING HUNGRY.

BUT WHEN HE ARRIVED, HE HAD ANOTHER SURPRISE.

HELLO!

THERE WERE NOW **MORE** OF HIS SISTER!

HELLO!

HELLO!

AAAAHHHH!

ACTUALLY, HE HAD BEEN AWAY FOR SO LONG, MOVING AT ALMOST THE SPEED OF LIGHT, THAT SIXTY YEARS HAD PASSED ON EARTH. HIS SISTER HAD HAD TRIPLETS, AND THOSE TRIPLETS HAD HAD OTHER TRIPLETS!

FORTUNATELY, THEY LIKED TO PLAY VIDEO GAMES, SO IT ALL WORKED OUT IN THE END.

THINGS YOU CAN TELL (YOUR **PARENTS** at the Dinner Table that will ☆**IMPRESS THEM**☆

THE UNIVERSE WAS ONCE SMALLER THAN A TINY DOT!

THE SUN IS SQUISHPLODING **ALL THE TIME!**

A BLACK HOLE IS A HOLE IN **SPACE!**

YOU CAN MAKE A BLACK HOLE OUT OF **ANYTHING!**

IN BILLIONS OF YEARS, THE SUN WILL GROW SO BIG, IT WILL EAT UP EARTH!

IF YOU FALL INTO A BLACK HOLE, YOU WILL PROBABLY NEVER GET OUT!

REMEMBER, EXPLAINING SOMETHING IS ONE OF THE BEST WAYS OF UNDERSTANDING IT!

EARTH IS THE ONLY PLANET IN THE SOLAR SYSTEM WITH LIQUID WATER ON IT!

MOST OF THE UNIVERSE IS MADE OF SPOOKY, MYSTERIOUS DARK MATTER AND DARK ENERGY!

ON SATURN, IT RAINS **DIAMONDS!**

THE UNIVERSE IS **SO BIG,** WE CAN'T SEE ALL OF IT!

WHOA.

IF YOU STAND UP, TIME MOVES SLOWER FOR YOUR FEET THAN FOR YOUR HEAD!

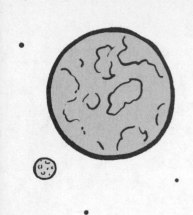

WANT TO LEARN MORE?

Check out these websites and books:

NASA for kids: spaceplace.nasa.gov

American Museum of Natural History:
amnh.org/explore/ology/astronomy

European Space Agency for kids: esa.int/kids

Astrophysics for Young People in a Hurry by Neil deGrasse
Tyson. New York: Norton Young Readers, 2019.

Outer Space by Ken Jennings. New York: Little Simon, 2014.

Also, go to your local library! Just ask for resources or
books about space and the universe. I'm pretty sure they
have a ton of them.

SO. MANY. BOOKS!

ACKNOWLEDGMENTS

Big thanks to the scientists who helped make sure everything in this book is right, including Andrew Howard (the real Dr. Howard!), Katie Mack, Phyllis Whittlesey, David Cinabro, Julie Comerford, and Matt Siegler. Thanks to all the kids and parents who read drafts of this book, including Linda Simensky, Mateo, Layla, the Scotts, Oliver's D&D group, the Rodriguezes, the Howards, the Phippards, and the Woldeits. Huge thanks to Howard Reeves and the Abrams team, and to Seth Fishman and the Gernert team. Thanks to Suelika, Elinor, and Oliver (the real Oliver!), who are my inspiration and unofficial cowriters.

JORGE CHAM is a blockbuster, Emmy-nominated creator of many things, from the celebrated PBS show *Elinor Wonders Why* to the bestselling adult nonfiction book *We Have No Idea* to the hit podcast *Daniel & Jorge Explain the Universe*, to the popular webcomic PHD Comics. He is, without a doubt, an EXPERT on explaining things about the world in interesting, fun ways. Jorge obtained a PhD in robotics from Stanford University and used to do research in a brain lab at Caltech, where he was an instructor. He's the proud dad of the real Oliver, who inspired this book and many of the things that happen in it. Originally from Panama, he lives with his family in South Pasadena, California.

INDEX